Gloria watched his smooth brown throat. "Do you want another one? Though I don't think you should drink it so fast," Gloria could have bitten her tongue out for sounding like a mother hen.

"No, thanks. Maybe later." Matt's dark chocolate eyes twinkled at her, as if he knew her thoughts and strolled back to labor in her yard. He turned to look at her. "So, did she die?"

"No, I divorced her, or, I divorced her son, my ex."

"Ah." Matt smiled and went back to work.

What did that smile mean, Gloria wondered? And "Ah". What did that mean?

She busied herself in the kitchen, getting the chicken ready. Where was Gordy? Surely, taking a class off his schedule didn't take so long. Did it? Well, he had said the line to see the counselor was long.

Once she put the chicken in the oven to bake, Gloria grabbed a novel she had been trying to finish reading. The author wrote long boring speeches about the universe and the duties of a woman. She was ready to throw the book against the nearest wall. Still, she hated to stop reading a book before she finished it. However boring the book might have been in parts, soon, engrossed in it, she almost missed Matt's knock.

"Gloria?" Matt called and rapped on the patio door again.

She jumped to her feet, laying the book on the coffee table. Without thinking, her hands went up to smooth her hair and gather it up more tightly in the gold clip she wore. She opened the door and stepped outside.

"So, what do you want to do about these roses? Mow 'em down, too?" Matt asked.

Too Late For Romance?

by

L. M. Gonzalez

Too Late For Romance

Cover Art by *Tamra Westberry*

The Wild Rose Press
PO Box 708
Adams Basin, NY 14410-0706
Visit us at www.thewildrosepress.com

Publishing History
First Last Rose Of Summer Rose Edition, 2007
Print ISBN 1-60154-155-4

Published in the United States of America

DEDICATION

Dedicated to my parents, Alberto M. and Tomasa Morales: To my dad, for always providing for his family, thus allowing me to pursue my dreams. To my mom, for teaching me to read my first words and for showing me, by example, that a woman could as easily wield a mop as she could a hammer.

Chapter One

I have high blood pressure.
Life had caught up with her. Gloria knew it was
bound to happen given the battering she had given her
body through the years—burgers, fries, and alcohol—
almost on a daily basis.

The chaos at work had settled a bit so she had taken
this beautiful early August day off from Home Nursing,
the home health agency where she worked. Her rose
garden was in sad shape and she needed to do something
about it. She threw the red roses she had just cut in the
tub of cool water she'd placed on a wooden dining room
chair. She had seen it done in a home and garden TV
show recently. This was a way to revive them. She didn't
have a green thumb, but she loved being among flowers
and plants. Last spring she planted her garden. Last
summer her roses had died. This year she was determined
her garden would bloom and she'd enjoy cut flowers in her
house. For a time, her roses had blossomed, but now in
the hot August days they were dying. Gloria looked out
the window at her roses.

She knew beautiful living things would perk her up.
Suddenly, she felt old—and unattractive. She had never
been a great beauty, but she had always been able to look
herself in the mirror and at least like the woman she saw
staring back. Lately, that woman looked old. Wrinkles at
the corners of her lips—laugh lines. *Yeah, right.* Too many
gray hairs; which she'd dyed. Had six weeks really gone
by already? Or were her gray roots taking over her
brunette hair?

"Mom, where are you?" Gordy asked, coming in from
registering for school.

Gordon Daniel Amaya, her baby, was about to begin
his senior year in high school. She couldn't believe it. No
longer a baby anymore, he was taller than she, thin, but
muscular, as he loved to lift weights.

1

"In the kitchen." She placed the roses in a vase of water, where she had thrown in a penny, apparently an inhibitor of bacteria. Another tip from the home and garden show.

"I got my schedule. They messed up. Chemistry is still on there. I just spent my whole summer taking this course. I'm not taking it again." Gordy threw the schedule on the large wooden dining table and hitched up the jeans he wore mid-hip. He tossed his cap on a nearby chair in the adjacent living room. She shook her head at his unruly curly black hair, which he painstakingly smoothed out every morning.

Heaving a sigh, and refraining from nagging him about how he wore his pants, Gloria asked, "Didn't you talk to the counselor?"

"The line was too long,"

She looked at her son, "Gordy..."

"I know. I'll go back in a minute." He dropped into the textured brown and white fabric recliner.

She finished arranging the roses in the vase. "Doesn't that look pretty? Maybe they'll live a little longer now."

Flipping through the channels with the remote, Gordy barely glanced at the flowers. "Yeah."

Gloria inhaled the aroma of the roses, tart and sweet at the same time. Nature couldn't be duplicated. She loved the smell of fresh roses, but not in perfumes, candles or potpourri where the scent was always so strong.

Taking the vase from the dining room table, she placed the arrangement on the coffee table. Once she removed the newspapers, soda cans and water bottles, the roses looked nice. She sat on the matching sofa adjacent to the recliner to admire the flowers.

"Where's the idiot?" Gordy asked, having settled on a rap music video station.

"You know, I gave you boys perfectly good names. Why don't you ever use them?" Gloria sighed and frowned at her son for calling his brother names. But they were always doing that. Terms of affection, she supposed. But if her sister, Lynda, ever called her an idiot, she'd probably cry. They had always enjoyed a close relationship. Girls, at least from her experience, tended to be more sensitive about name-calling.

"So, where is the beep?" Gordy changed the channel.

Gloria gave up and answered, "At the college. I hope all goes well for him. Yesterday, he said he got horrid news. You know how your brother is with phrases."

What Dex meant was that he might not be eligible for any more loans to finish out his college career. Since he had applied late for financial aid, his loans had been delayed. The delay had not been the only bad news. There had been so many challenges through the years as a single parent. Now her health was in trouble. She had talked to her sister about her high blood pressure. Lynda had advised her not to tell her sons. She felt dishonest not telling them, but she didn't want them to worry either.

"The gardener is coming today," Gloria said.

"Aw..." Gordy began.

"Well, it's not like you're going to have to help him," she laughed and adjusted her gold wire frame glasses. She pushed back a loose strand of raven hair behind her ear.

"I know, but he makes a lot of racket with the lawn mower."

"Put earplugs on. Unless, you're going to watch TV?"

"No, I want to play that new video game I bought."

Gordy had recently begun a part-time job at a print and copy shop and was happy to have spending money. She had advised him to also save money for a rainy day. Of course, he looked at her as if she had grown horns.

"I'll watch TV. Tell me when the gardener comes. I'll go back to fix my schedule. Or maybe I can wait until the first day of school?"

Gloria noticed his hopeful look. "Gordy, you know what a mess that will be. Go today."

As she said that, the doorbell rang. She knew it was the gardener, so she shouted out, "I'll meet you in the backyard."

She looked down at herself—faded jeans, old T-shirt, dark hair in a clip. Nothing that Wayne Simmons hadn't seen before. He barely looked at her anyway, always eager to get started with her yard which had been overgrown with weeds and out of control grass until she had hired him. He came like clockwork every other week during the summer, monthly, in the winter.

She slid the patio door open and stepped outside. "Hi, Wayne," she called out as she closed the door and turned toward the gate.

Gloria stopped in her tracks when she saw a strange man walking through the tall wooden gate, pushing his lawn mower, muscles standing out on his upper arms. He wore jeans and a blue work shirt. His gray cap, which bore the emblem of the local basketball team, covered black hair.

"Hello, I'm Matt Cerda. Wayne got backed up and called me in to help him out."

Gloria stared. He looked so male. Well, of course, he did, she told herself. He was a man. What a ridiculous thought! "Uh...yes. I mean, I'm Gloria Amaya, but you probably know that already." She felt herself blushing. When was the last time she had done that?

He pushed up his cap with a long slender brown finger and gazed at her with dark brown eyes that seemed to see all her flaws, spreading hips and all. "Wayne told me you needed the yard mowed and something about a flower garden?"

Gloria swallowed, felt her pulse racing and looked toward her rose bushes, pink and red and brown and black. She knew roses shouldn't be brown and leaves shouldn't be black. "Do you know about flower gardens?"

He pulled a business card from his shirt pocket. "Here's my card. When it comes to flowers, I'm an artist."

Gloria took it and read: *Mateo Cerda, If It's Green, I Can Grow It, Lawns, Trees, Flowers*. Simple, yet direct. "How long have you been in business?"

"All my life. I started mowing lawns at ten years old. You would have cried at how sweet I looked pushing that big lawn mower. Sometimes, the grass would be taller than me," Matt grinned.

Gloria laughed out loud, but quickly lowered her eyes to the card again, fearing he'd think she was crazy. Or worse yet, he'd think she was flirting.

She remembered Gordy had to go see the counselor about his schedule. Excusing herself to Matt, she opened the patio door and called out a reminder to her son.

"Man! Just when my game was getting good, too."

Gordy's voice came from inside the house.

Before she could answer, he had slammed the front door. "My son. He's a senior this year."

She heard Gordy's car start and the speakers blaring out, making the neighborhood tremble.

"Ah, to be a teenager again," Matt said.

"Oh no, not me! Well, okay, but only to be young again." She wished she could take the statement back. Why had she said that? Almost as if she was fishing for a compliment.

"You probably look just like you did when you were a teenager."

Gloria knew he was teasing her, but for a second, she did feel like a giddy teenager flirting with a boy she liked.

"Just like you do, huh?" She stared at his muscled arms.

"I wish," Matt said and touched his stomach, "not as flat as I used to be. Or as fit." He leaned on the lawn mower, his arms crossed over the handle.

That may be, Gloria thought, but those muscles…too bad he's wearing a shirt.

"Better get started. The sun is relentless once it gets higher up in the sky," Matt said.

Gloria looked at her watch. 9:45 in the morning. "Okay, I'll leave you alone. But, I do want to talk to you about my roses."

"What's the matter with them?" He walked over to the rosebushes along the fence. "Oh, I see."

She followed him. "They're dying," Gloria frowned. "I picked a few this morning to try and save them."

Matt stood still, looking at the roses, then at her. "I see."

"Can you help me?"

It seemed as if he were a million miles away. What could he be thinking about?

"I have to mow the yard. I'll call you after awhile."

Gloria felt dismissed, almost as if they'd gone out on a date and now at its end he'd said he'd call, but she knew he wouldn't. Which was a foolish thought. She must go back inside the house. The morning sun was making her silly. Besides, her home and garden show was about to start.

As she slid the patio door closed, she watched Matt pull the cord to start the lawn mower. A warm feeling infused her veins. Before she could turn away, he turned and saw her at the door. Flustered, she closed the curtains over the door. Oh my. Gloria fanned herself with her hands. Relentless heat, huh?

From the patio door, she stared at the roses in the vase. What had Matt seen when he looked at her roses? He had seemed disturbed. However, he did like to grow things. It was his business, after all.

Gloria walked through the dining room to the kitchen to make a glass of instant tea and remove a breakfast bar from the box on top of the microwave. Her thoughts kept straying toward Matt. She heard the whirr of the lawn mower outside. She might not be able to hear her TV show, the second episode of the morning, the time when she usually ate breakfast. She loved to see how the hostess made things in her arts and crafts room, how she cooked and baked such delicious dishes and how she decorated the different rooms in her house. Gloria always wished she had more patience to do all those things. Her decorating ran more to hanging pictures of her family on the walls and setting out candle holders.

The apple flavored breakfast bar tasted delicious. Umm! Tea and a sweet—she loved this breakfast. She would have preferred a waffle, and her usual two glasses of tea in the morning. But now she had to limit herself. Her doctor advised her that if she was one of those people who must have their caffeine in the morning to only have one serving and no more. That was a hardship for someone who previously drank gallons of tea during the day. Now, she drank water. It wasn't that bad, though. Water was her sister's beverage of choice so she could get used to it, too.

Gloria glanced at the TV and saw the delicious chocolate cake. *I'd sure like a piece of that cake instead of this stupid breakfast bar. No! I must not think like that.*

Two weeks ago she thought she was going to die. One of the nurses at work, Annie, her friend ever since her boys were little, had taken her blood pressure. It was 144 over 104. Gloria knew that was bad. The norm for her was usually 120 over 80. If she had collapsed on the spot, she wouldn't have been surprised. The next day it was better, but not much. By the end of the week, she had gone to the doctor, who told her, "You're not leaving here without some blood pressure medicine."

Later on that day, her right arm had started to feel numb. Completely scared out of her wits, she had rushed to the doctor's office. Her blood pressure stabilized, but Dr. DeLeon advised her to take it easy. So she went home and got into bed where ridiculous ideas invaded her mind.

I'm going to have a stroke. I'm going to die and I'm not ready. Gordy is going to be a senior. Dex is in his last year in college. Admittedly, maybe, they don't need me as much, but they wouldn't be happy if I dropped dead. And I want to see them get married and have children. I want to... Oh, I have so much more to do.

She'd eat this damn breakfast bar and limit her tea and exercise and lose weight. She listened to the whirr of the lawn mower. Maybe, now, she'd have more incentive. Gloria shook her head to clear her thoughts. He was probably married and had a houseful of kids. *A man like that! Like what, Gloria? He's just a man.*

On a commercial, she sneaked a peak out the window. When Wayne mowed her lawn, she always opened the curtains by the dining room, which overlooked the backyard. Today, she didn't, feeling self-conscious. She tried to look out without moving the curtain too much and couldn't see a thing. Damn! He probably knew she was standing there like a peeping Tom. Oh wait, peeping Toms looked in, not out. She laughed and covered her mouth quickly. Two weeks ago, she thought she'd die from a stroke. This week, she could go insane.

"Mrs. Amaya," Matt called out and rapped on the patio door.

Gloria jumped, but calmed herself before she opened it.

"Call me Gloria," she said.

"I'm going to go mow the front, edge the sidewalks and trim the bushes. Then, we'll look at the roses."

"Do you like roses?"

"Yeah. The ladies sure like receiving them."

His grin made her stomach turn a somersault and she cleared her throat. "You looked funny when you were studying them earlier."

Matt turned away and started pushing the lawn mower around to the front. "Your apple tree needs to be trimmed, too. Would you like me to do that?"

Would you like me to do that? Gloria wondered how those words would sound if he said them to her in bed. Oh my God! What had she just thought? She couldn't look at him.

"Mrs. Amaya?"

"We'll talk about it after you look at the roses."

She wanted to remind him to call her Gloria, but after that awful thought she just wanted to go back inside her house. What was she thinking? She was a forty-something woman, for heaven's sake, with two grown sons. Mid-forties, as Lynda liked to remind her since she was seven years younger. Gloria's time for romance and men had ended. She had no time—or inclination for this. Or did she?

She looked at the TV. The hostess said something about learning to share likes and dislikes in home décor with your significant other, and they could have a harmonious and romantic time. Gloria changed the channel in disgust. Romance again! That was for the young people—like her older son, Dex. Not her—with her health problems, gray roots and spreading hips. Or was it?

Gordy would be back soon. She must get her thoughts in order. Lunch—she would think about what to make for lunch. Opening the freezer, she saw frozen pizza, hamburger meat, chicken. What could she make? Now that she couldn't have burgers, fries or pizza, that's what she most wanted. She decided to bake the chicken with potatoes for the boys and throw in broccoli and carrots for herself. As she started to prepare it, the doorbell rang. Had Gordy forgotten his key?

Gloria wiped her hands on a towel, ambled to the front door and opened it. Matt stood in the doorway. His face glistened with sweat, grass covered his shoes and lower part of his jeans—and he looked so good to her. The smell of newly cut grass and the gas the lawn mower used filled the air. But the scent of this man standing in front of her—so different from her sons—assailed her senses.

"Could I trouble you for some water? My cooler leaked. I brought some water, but it's all over the bed of my truck."

Bed. Yes, a bed would be good. Oh!

"Mrs. Amaya?"

"Of course, you can have some…"

"Water," he finished for her.

"Yes, water. I'll get it for you. And call me Gloria. Mrs. Amaya is my mother-in-law."

Gloria pulled a cold bottle of water from the refrigerator, strolled back and handed it to Matt. "*Was* my mother-in-law."

"Did she die?" Matt asked before he drank the bottle of water in one long thirst-quenching gulp.

Gloria watched his smooth brown throat. "Do you want another one? Though I don't think you should drink it so fast," Gloria could have bitten her tongue out for sounding like a mother hen.

"No, thanks. Maybe later." Matt's dark chocolate eyes twinkled at her, as if he knew her thoughts and strolled back to labor in her yard. He turned to look at her. "So, did she die?"

"No, I divorced her, or, I divorced her son, my ex."

"Ah." Matt smiled and went back to work.

What did that smile mean, Gloria wondered? And "Ah". What did that mean?

She busied herself in the kitchen, getting the chicken ready. Where was Gordy? Surely, taking a class off his schedule didn't take so long. Did it? Well, he had said the line to see the counselor was long.

Once she put the chicken in the oven to bake, Gloria grabbed a novel she had been trying to finish reading. The author wrote long boring speeches about the universe and the duties of a woman. She was ready to throw the book against the nearest wall. Still, she hated to stop reading a book before she finished it. However boring the book might have been in parts, soon, engrossed in it, she almost missed Matt's knock.

"Gloria?" Matt called and rapped on the patio door again.

She jumped to her feet, laying the book on the coffee table. Without thinking, her hands went up to smooth her hair and gather it up more tightly in the gold clip she wore. She opened the door and stepped outside.

"So, what do you want to do about these roses? Mow 'em down, too?" Matt asked.

Chapter Two

"No, I don't want to mow them down," Gloria's mouth dropped open.

"You know, with your mouth like that, it makes me want to come closer and see how mine would fit over it."

"What?" Gloria would have kept her mouth wide open, if she hadn't been so aghast at what he had just said. He was her gardener. A stranger. Forget that she had been having sexy thoughts about him all morning.

"Sorry, couldn't help myself," Matt smiled. "Now, about your roses..."

"You can't say something like that and just...just..."

"Just what? Come on. What do you want to say?" He walked closer to her.

"I bet women all over San Antonio want to slap you, don't they?"

"No, just my wife." He teased her.

"Your wife! You're married and you're saying these things to me?" Gloria glared at him.

"No, I'm not married. I should have said my ex-wife. She'd like to slap me, probably kill me, too."

Gloria crossed her arms over her chest. "I wonder why."

"Me, too." Matt stood still by the roses again. His eyes seemed to cloud over with sadness.

"What is it with you and the roses? Don't you like roses?"

"I love 'em. My mom used to grow the most beautiful roses in our backyard—all colors, red, pink, yellow and white. She's the one who taught me how to take care of green living things." Matt gazed into the distance, toward the neighbor's house. "She also grew an herb garden. You know the kind older ladies have with rosemary, cilantro, basil and oregano of course."

"Tea made with oregano—good for coughs and sore throats," Gloria remembered.

11

"With honey and lemon," Matt grinned.

"Better than cough syrup any day." Gloria searched his face. "What happened to your mother?"

"She died." Matt walked away. Clearly, he did not want to talk about his mom.

Gloria could understand that. It had been twenty years since her mom had died and sometimes she still missed her dreadfully.

"So, what can you do for my roses?"

"First, we need to spray them. You've got black-spot."

"Black-spot? What is that?" Gloria looked at her roses; sure they were going to die in the next few seconds.

"It's a fungus. Most roses get them."

Gloria stooped to study her roses more closely. Straightening up, her apprehension must have shown in her face because Matt smiled and continued.

"It can be taken care of. I'll spray them with a fungicide. You also have mildew. That's what this white stuff on the leaves is. Another type of fungus."

"I thought that meant I watered them too much. So I stopped."

"That explains the dryness. We need to pinch off all the deadheads. They're draining the rest of the bush. Then, we'll cut off roses from each bush. That helps new buds to appear." Matt hunched down and removed his work glove. He probed the soil around the base of the rose bush. "We need to put down some fertilizer. Then, we'll see if they revive. It's getting hotter and hotter. It might be too late in the year. But, I'll try my best."

"Thank you." Gloria breathed a sigh of relief.

"Mom! The timer is going off!" Gordy yelled. *When did he get home? Did he overhear anything?* She noticed the partially closed patio door.

"Excuse me. I'll be right back. My son who yells is home." Gloria hurried toward the house.

"I'll be here," Matt waved to her.

As soon as Gloria stepped inside, she scolded. "Gordy, don't yell. I've got the gardener out there, for heaven's sake." She closed the patio door.

"Well, the timer went off. What are you making?"

"Chicken."

"Chicken?" Gordy asked, drawing out the word.

"Yes, with vegetables."

"Do we have macaroni and cheese?" He opened the cupboard above the stove.

"Gordy, I put potatoes in the chicken. That's enough starch."

"Aw, Mom. We need mac-and-cheese. I'll make it." Gordy pulled the box from the cupboard.

"Gordy, you know it's not that I don't want to make it for you."

"Come on, Mom. I'm exercising now and I don't eat as much at night." Her son grinned and gave her one of his rare hugs.

"Okay, okay. But only because you caught me in a good mood."

"Because of the yardman? He's not Wayne, is he?"

"No, Wayne was busy. He sent Matt. And he's a gardener, by the way."

Gordy grinned, "Matt, the gardener, huh?" And then he said, as he walked to his room, "I'm not calling him Dad."

Gloria laughed. "Who said you had to? He's just here to fix my roses." She took a pot out and filled it with water. She called out to Gordy, "By the way, did you take care of your schedule?"

"Yeah," Gordy called back.

"So they took Chemistry off?"

"I left a note."

I hope it's fixed by Monday.

Gloria set the pot of water on the stove and turned on the heat. She snuck over to the dining room and peeped through the crack in the curtains. Where was Matt? She couldn't see him.

She heard a rap on the patio door and almost jumped out of her skin. Composing herself, she slid open the patio door. "Are you finished?"

Matt told her, "I'm going to have to come back tomorrow. I need more fertilizer. Unless, you don't mind if I return this evening?" His work shirt hung over his left shoulder and in the white muscle T-shirt he wore, he took her breath away. Muscled, dark brown arms, shining with sweat.

Gloria swallowed. She couldn't find her voice.

Matt stared at her, "Gloria?"

"Uh, yeah. Sure. Come back this evening. I'll be here."

He turned away, but not before she glimpsed a certain something in his dark gaze. Something like he wanted to flirt with her, but couldn't.

The heat, she told herself. Nothing more. He is just the gardener, as she had told Gordy.

"Mom! The mac-and-cheese!" Gordy yelled.

"Oh!" Gloria looked toward the stove and watched Gordy dump the macaroni in, then turned to Matt. "See you tonight."

Matt waved at her as he gathered up his equipment and tools.

"How long were you going to boil the water before you started cooking? I'm starving. What were you doing?"

Gloria opened the refrigerator and removed the gallon of milk and butter.

"Matt is coming back this evening. He ran out of fertilizer for my roses."

"Your roses? What's up with your roses?"

"They're dying." Gloria turned to rinse some dishes in the sink.

"Like last year."

"Yes, and I'm not going to let it happen again."

"It's too hot to grow anything in San Antonio."

"No, it's not. I'm going to prove you wrong. Besides, it's not the heat. It's fungus." Gloria looked out the window at her roses and remembered Matt would return this evening.

The doorbell rang and rang, then came a jangle of keys and the lock turning.

"The wuss is home." Gordy went to greet his brother with a punch to the stomach and more name-calling.

Dex dignified his little brother's greeting with a return punch and dubious endearments.

"Will you two ever grow up?" Gloria placed her hands on her waist. Her older son was as tall as his younger brother, but a tad heavier, though just as muscular. Dex liked to workout, too.

"Hi, Mom," Dex grabbed her around the back of her neck and gave her a slobbery kiss.

"Hold her, wuss!" Gordy yelled.

"No, come on, guys!" Gloria giggled. "Not today."

She returned to the kitchen when Dex let her go. Usually, she and her boys indulged in a mock punching match—their way of coming together after a long day apart. Today, though, she had other things on her mind— or rather someone. And he was coming back tonight.

Should she dress up? No. They were going to be in the garden. He'd notice and she'd be so embarrassed. Besides, he wasn't attracted to her in spite of his teasing.

Why had he said his wife wanted to kill him? What had he done to her? Why was he divorced? Did he have kids?

She shook her head, telling herself to stop thinking so much. Too much baggage came with relationships at her age. How could they possibly…?

"I finally cleared up my financial aid," Dex said.

Her ears perked up. "Good. How'd you manage it?"

"I got what's called a 'last opportunity loan' plus my $500 book voucher. The books will probably cost that much."

"Well, I'm glad. Only two more semesters to go and you'll have your degree in graphic design."

"I hope so."

"Hey, man, look at this rap video. The one I told you about." Gordy pressed the volume button on the remote control.

Gloria glanced at the TV—half-naked women again. "Why don't they ever have other kinds of videos? Different song, same video."

Gordy frowned. His expression showed that clearly, she didn't understand.

Turning away, she said, "Come and eat." Gloria served the plates of food. "Turn the TV down a bit so we can talk."

While eating, Gloria told both boys the gardener would return later tonight.

"What kind of a yardman comes back in the evening?" Dex asked.

"Matt does," Gordy grinned.

"Matt? What happened to Wayne? Who is this character?" Dex frowned.

Gloria laughed. "Dex, really. It's for my roses." She tasted the chicken and vegetables. "This is wonderful. Wayne couldn't come today so he asked Matt to help him."

Dex smiled gently. "Your roses."

Gloria knew her son understood. He had found her crying in her garden last year because they had died.

"Matt is trying to save them. A lot of them are dying already. Wilting, getting brown, like me, only I'm going gray."

"And wilting?" Gordy teased

"Yes." Gloria continued eating. "I have to save them. They also have fungus. But Matt sprayed them with something."

"I'm going out with my friends tonight, remember, Mom?" Dex said. "It's Tony's birthday."

Gloria nodded. "I remember." Dex had been friends with Tony since elementary school.

"I'll go to the movies with Will," Gordy said.

"Ya'll don't have to leave," Gloria suddenly had to take a deep breath. She felt the attraction for Matt and the anticipation. She remembered she had an unopened bottle of wine in the refrigerator. Hadn't touched it since she'd been diagnosed with hypertension. Damn. She hated that word. The elderly Home Nursing patients contended with that disease. Not her.

The boys helped her clean the table and put the dishes in the sink, then went to their room to play video games. Gloria picked up the book she left on the coffee table earlier, but she couldn't keep her mind on the story. She reiterated to herself that Matt was only coming back for her roses. That's all. Her sons had made their plans and she would be by herself and her own devices. Given her attraction to Matt, she didn't believe leaving her alone was such a good idea.

Before she knew it, she dozed off while reading her book and woke up to hear her sons getting ready to go out. Their voices teasing each other about what they would wear filled her ears. She smiled.

"I'll see you later, Mom," Gordy said.

"Is Will here already?" Gloria asked; biting her tongue at the sight of Gordy's hanging pants.

"Yeah. He's coming around the corner. He just

called." Gordy waved his cell.

"Be careful, boys!" Gloria shouted, as both Dex and Gordy left. Dex, in his black truck he wanted to replace and Gordy in Will's car. She waved from the door as they drove away.

Anticipation reared its head again. Gloria wanted to take a shower, but it was seven o'clock. Matt should arrive soon, before sunset.

She'd just put on some clean jeans, a nicer T-shirt. Just to smell fresher, not be seductive. He probably dated someone already anyway. He was just coming for her roses.

For a wild moment, Gloria felt as if all she needed was some tender loving care, as the nurses at work liked to give their elderly patients. A little TLC would revive her roses too.

Gloria should dye away her gray roots. Allow herself to bloom by getting rid of all those thoughts about wrinkles and spreading hips.

She walked into her bedroom, threw her hair clip on the dresser, and changed her clothes. As she looked in the mirror, she dabbed on just a touch of lipstick. Lynda had given it to her. The lipstick didn't have too deep a color. There. She couldn't even tell she wore it. She brushed her hair and let it hang loose.

The doorbell rang. Her heart beat rapidly. Placing a hand to her chest, she wondered if a stroke could be induced by getting over-excited. She couldn't make love with hypertension. Could she? Oh, for goodness' sake...

She went to open the front door. And he wasn't there. Where did he go? A white truck with his name, *Mateo Cerda*, in green letters on the door was parked in front of her house. She heard a rapping on the patio door. Grinning, she closed the front door and ran to the patio.

Calm down, she told herself.

She slid the door open and saw Matt bending down to add fertilizer to her roses.

Please stay alive, she pleaded. In that moment, she asked the universe to keep her happiness alive as well as her roses.

Matt turned to look at her and smiled, "Hi. Are you going out?"

Damn. He had noticed.

"No. I don't think so."

His smile grew wider. He hadn't changed his clothes. Of course not, he was working.

She fidgeted with her hair, realized she didn't have her clip and didn't meet his eyes. "Maybe to a movie. Later."

The backyard was in shade now. The house faced west so in the evenings the backyard was a nice place to be—at least when it wasn't summer.

"Can I help you?" Gloria volunteered.

"No, I'm done." Matt groaned as he straightened from his squatting position. "I'm tired. It's been a long day."

"Do you want some water?"

He was leaving already. She couldn't let him go yet. Not giving him time to answer, she hurried inside for the water and returned.

"Come sit down." She led him to the patio table. They sat in chairs covered with green and white striped cushions.

"Hey, these are comfortable chairs," Matt said.

"Maybe it's just because you're tired?" She lifted herself part way up then plopped back down on the plushy cushions. And was suddenly conscious of her breasts swaying with the movement. She noticed Matt's eyes on her. "They are comfortable. I like to sit out here and read, look at my garden, think."

"Just like my mom. She loved being outside with her plants." Matt turned toward her garden. Then, he looked down and wrung his hands.

"Matt..." Gloria wondered what disturbed him.

"Her herbs, especially." Matt tasted a sip of water. "I remember the times she'd go out to her garden to pick out some herb that supposedly was good for anything that ailed us. We took to keeping our sicknesses to ourselves to avoid those herbal teas and hot packs."

Gloria laughed. "My mom was like that, too. Only she didn't grow her own. My aunt gave them to her. Yerba Buena. Remember that one? Supposedly good for stomach aches. Mom would make a hot poultice with it. *Tia* didn't grow them either, but she bought them. She had a flower garden, though." She stopped her babbling.

"Is your son home?" Matt took another drink of water.

"Actually, I have two sons, but no. They made plans with their friends."

"You're alone." He grinned, "Come with me. I want to show you something."

Gloria walked with him past the roses and stopped under her tree, which he had said needed trimming.

"What do you want to show me? I hope my roses will be alright. I couldn't bear it..."

Matt put his hands on her shoulders and pulled her closer to him. "I can't bear not to touch you anymore."

Gloria's heart beat faster. Had it jumped up to her throat? Because she couldn't swallow—or breathe. She saw his face coming nearer. And then his lips were on hers, gently, caressing them, first the top one, then the bottom.

She sighed, then deepened the kiss and put her arms around him. He was taller than she was, but not overly so.

His kisses—wet, intimate, overwhelming. And she didn't want them to stop. Her legs weakened under her. He held her up and stopped the kiss to caress her neck and ears and cheeks.

"Matt, someone will see us," Gloria gasped.

"Let them." And he continued to kiss her.

"These are my neighbors." She forced her lips away from his.

"Do you want to go inside?"

No, she wasn't ready for that. She had just met him. She wasn't twenty years old, after all.

"I can't."

"I'm sorry."

"Please don't apologize." Gloria pleaded.

"I'm pushy that way. When I see something I want, I take." He grinned, so she knew he was teasing.

"How many have you taken?" Gloria asked and wished the ground under her roses would open up and swallow her.

"Don't get the idea that I go from yard to yard seducing housewives like some sex-crazed lawn man," Matt said.

Gloria tried to say something, anything, but her throat felt dry.

"I liked you the minute I saw you." Matt stared at her with his arms crossed over his chest.

"Really?" Gloria felt like a silly schoolgirl.

"Really."

"Why does your wife want to kill you?"

Matt nodded. "I get it. You want the sordid details."

"I suppose."

"I stopped paying her alimony a few months ago."

"You don't have to in Texas." Alimony? Her ex, Eddie Amaya, hadn't ever even paid her child support!

"I know, but I did. Mostly, because I didn't want her using the child support for herself." Matt touched one of the nearby red roses.

"You have kids?"

"Yeah, three girls."

"What are their names? How old are they?"

"Three daughters—Amber is twelve, Patsy, fifteen and Julia, seventeen. Do you want to see pictures?" Matt's hand went to his back pocket.

"Sure." *Three daughters?*

They walked back to the table. Gloria sat and took the pictures Matt handed her. As she looked at the images, she saw that two had black hair like Matt's, one had brown hair and wore glasses. "They're pretty."

"Yeah. Julia and Patsy got my black hair. Amber has brown hair." He looked at the pictures before he put them back in his wallet and slipped it into his pocket. "I divorced Angela because she cheated on me two years ago. And now the bozo is living with her, and I'm not supporting her anymore. That's why she wants to kill me."

"Her mistake."

"In not killing me?" Matt teased her.

"No. In cheating on you."

Matt grinned. "See, I knew there was a reason I liked you immediately. I'd better go. Need to shower and change out of these clothes."

"Okay. When will you be back?" Gloria wished he'd kiss her again. "For the roses."

"I'll be back Monday, in the evening. You work,

right?" Matt stood up, drinking the last of the water.

"Yes. I usually get home around six."

"See you then." Matt turned away, pushing the wheelbarrow with the fertilizer, then looked back at her. "Would you like to come with me while I change? I'll take you out to eat."

"I can't..."

"Why not?" Matt walked all the way back to her and kissed her without touching her. Just let her feel his lips on hers. When she tried to put her arms around him, he wouldn't let her.

"Would you like to know how I could make love to you just with my mouth?"

Chapter Three

"Oh." Gloria squeaked.

"Let's go."

"Okay." She agreed and stumbled inside the house while Matt gathered up his equipment and loaded it on his truck. Oh my! No one had ever kissed her like him. The image of her ex loomed in her mind. Yes, Eddie had kissed her breathless, but they had been so young and foolish. Matt's kisses were from a mature man, a man who had been hurt, but had survived—just as she had, without being unfaithful in his marriage. And he was waiting for her.

As Gloria wrote a note to her boys, turned off the lights and locked doors, she couldn't believe what she intended to do. How could she? She had just met this man. But Wayne knew him. He wouldn't send her a depraved man, would he? Of course not.

The phone rang. The caller ID indicated Dex's cell number.

"Hi, Dex. What's up?"

"Just checking in. We're at the movies, too. Gordy and Will already went in. Are you okay?"

"Yes. I'm going out. I left you a note. I didn't want to call you while you were with your friend."

"Who are you going out with?" Dex asked.

She could picture the frown on his face. "Matt."

"The yardman?" Gloria could hear his surprise over the phone.

"Yes, and he's waiting for me. I'd better go."

"Be careful, Mom. You don't even know him."

"No, but Wayne does. And I know Wayne."

"Still..."

"I know. I won't be too late. And don't you be either."

Maybe she should call Wayne. No, she couldn't. Without thinking too much about it and feeling pressured because Matt waited, she quickly dialed Wayne's number.

His wife, Tanya, answered. Gloria almost groaned. She loved her, but Tanya loved to talk.

"Hi, Gloria. Did Matt find your house okay?"

"Yes, he did. He's going to try and save my roses." Gloria glanced at the door. Matt waited outside and her heart seemed to turn over inside her.

"*Ay Dios*, not again. Why, Gloria? You cried for days last year."

"This year is going to be different."

"I hope so, for your sake. Though Matt is great with flowers. Got my sorry garden blooming. Not even Wayne could do anything with it. He tried and tried and just made it worse and me madder. Did you want Wayne? He's taking a shower. Tired out, the poor baby! Hey, Matt is a good egg. I'm so glad he got rid of that Angela. Nothing but trouble, that slut. Matt needs a good woman, a nice one, like you, my friend."

Gloria felt happiness swell inside. Matt was a "good egg", greater praise Tanya couldn't give a person. But then, an idea occurred to her. "Tanya, did you—?"

Her friend interrupted, "I mean it. You've been alone too long."

"Tanya?"

"Plus, he's a great gardener."

Gloria gave up. If Tanya didn't want to divulge information, not even torture would make her do it. "Well...tell Wayne I'll talk to him later. And thank him for sending Matt over."

As she said that, Gloria wondered if she meant thanks for her roses, or for herself. Both; definitely both.

"I sure will, honey."

Gloria hung up and raced outside.

When she got to the truck, Matt asked, "Change your mind?"

"No, my son called. And I had something to do... Please forgive me."

"It's going to cost you." He pulled her into the truck and kissed her. Afterwards, he kept her near him as he started the truck and drove away. Music from a Tejano station filled the truck.

Gloria strapped the middle seatbelt on. "Do you dance?" She asked, as the sounds of a cumbia started. In a

23

cumbia, couples circled around the dance floor, moving their feet to the beat of the music and twirled, or were twirled by their partner as they went.

"Not much."

"Just my luck." Without volition, her body leaned toward his and the heat radiated between them.

The drive to Matt's house didn't take long once he got on the freeway. The traffic, thankfully, had died down. Matt pulled into the driveway of a small brick house. His yard bloomed beautifully. In the dimness, she could still see the green lawn. Flowers of all kinds, except for roses, grew along the sidewalk, which led up to the house.

"Your yard looks nice." Gloria said.

"Thanks. I've got a good gardener," he grinned.

Once inside the house, Matt got a beer and said, "Make yourself at home. I'll be quick. Do you want a beer?"

"No, I'd better not."

"There's some sodas and juice in the refrigerator. Wine, too. Help yourself. Glasses are in the cupboard." Matt waved in the direction of the kitchen.

When he left, Gloria looked around. He lived in a small house; living room, kitchen, dining, couple bedrooms—probably for when his daughters visited.

The furniture glowed with a dark wood polish. A faint odor of pine lingered in the air. The thought of Matt mopping his floors with Pinesol further endeared him to her. Over the fireplace, he displayed school pictures of his daughters. The older one was beautiful with long black hair and huge eyes. What was her name? Julia. Patsy looked sweet and tended toward the pudgy side. Amber wore glasses and brought back memories of herself in school. On a table by the brown leather sofa, she noticed a golf magazine and also a teen one. Next to the TV another small table featured play systems for video games.

Gloria wandered into the kitchen, opened the refrigerator and found the wine. She grabbed the bottle, opened the cupboard and found a wine glass. She poured some wine in—not too much—4 ounces. Her limit since she didn't want to mess with her blood pressure. Taking a sip, she put the bottle back. He had groceries. Not a typical bachelor. In the center of the dining room table a ceramic bowl with the initials J.C. took pride of place. Julia must have made it for him.

Back in the living room, she saw the doorway leading to what must be the master bedroom. Brazenly, she thought of going in there and waiting for him. What if he asked her to leave? What if he walked out naked and asked her to stay? She walked toward the bedroom, but then she heard the shower shutting off. She made a beeline for the stereo nearby. She pushed the button and a country-western station sang out.

"I can do the two-step." Matt entered the room, towel drying his hair, his tanned arm muscles bunching with the movement. He'd dressed in clean jeans and another one of those white muscle T-shirts.

Gloria almost choked on the wine she had just sipped. She put her glass down on a nearby table and stepped up to him leaning in to kiss him. He pulled her close, taking the initiative away from her. Her blood raced through her body and filled her with a sensation of warmth and languor.

"If we don't leave now, we'll never make it to the restaurant," Matt said.

"I don't care." She leaned into him to keep standing. Her eyes closed; she wanted this feeling to last forever.

"I'd rather stay here, too." Matt kissed her once more—quickly. "But you do care." He pulled on a shirt, then took her hand and led her outside to the truck.

As the engine revved to life, Matt asked, "What do you like?"

Gloria stared, wondering what he meant. Oh, he's talking about food. "Anything, except seafood."

"Bummer. That's my favorite."

Gloria smiled. "Which restaurant do you like? Do they have anything besides seafood?"

"Moe's Seafood?" He named a local restaurant she knew.

Gloria twisted her mouth in thought. "I can have a grilled chicken salad or sandwich. They also have a beef kabob. But they take longer with those." *And I shouldn't eat them anyway.*

"I can wait." His dark gaze settled on her lips.

Gloria shivered, tingling sensations ran up and down

her body. "No, I'd better have a salad. I think they sell chicken Caesar." She changed the subject as Matt's eyes lingered on her. "So, tell me more about your gardening."

"I started years ago. After I graduated from high school, I decided not to go to college. I wanted to work and earn money. Coming from a large family and all that."

"How large?"

"Five sisters and two brothers."

"Where are you in that?" *A huge family. What kind of people were they? And would they like her?*

"I'm the fourth among the sisters." Matt maneuvered his truck around a slow-moving white panel truck.

"So, your brothers are younger." Gloria glanced at him quickly, then turned to watch traffic.

"Yeah."

"Do they live in San Antonio?"

"Yes, all of them. We try to get together for as many birthdays and holidays as we can."

"My family and I try to do the same."

Matt returned to the subject of school. "I knew I could have applied for a grant to go to college."

"That's what I did."

Matt nodded, "But like I said, I wanted to earn money. Throughout school, in the summers, I mowed lawns and I always helped my mom in the garden, so I learned about flowers and plants. I decided to open a gardening and landscaping business. I've been doing this for thirty years now. Usually, I don't go to the homes to do the actual work anymore. I go to supervise the new guys. Wayne insisted I go to your house myself. Seemed kinda weird at the time. But, I'm glad I did." His glance settled on her a second before he turned his attention back to driving.

"Me, too." Gloria now knew Tanya's ulterior motive in Wayne's sending Matt to her house. But, somehow also felt happy about it.

"Besides, I hired a new guy who didn't show. Kinda concerned about him. Seemed to want to work. I'll check on him later." Matt gave her a quick glance as he changed lanes. "What about you? What do you do?"

"I work in home health care as a secretary. For a long time now, ten years. It's getting old. I want to try something new. Like work in a bookstore or library."

"You like books, huh?"

"Yes. Do you read?" Gloria asked.

"Sometimes. It's hard for me to sit down and read a book. I'd rather wait for the movie. I read the newspaper on a daily basis."

"My sons read the newspaper too and read the news on the web. And they also claim they read books." Gloria grinned.

The drive through San Antonio's freeways didn't take long. Gloria marveled at the ease of their conversation. Matt drove in to the restaurant parking lot. "I hope we don't have a long wait."

"We can have a drink and talk." Gloria suggested.

As she walked into the restaurant with Matt, the smell of frying fish assailed her.

Clinking glasses and loud voices filled the air. The hostess informed Matt of a thirty-minute wait. Matt gave his name. They stepped into the adjacent bar. He ordered a beer and she ordered a lemon-lime soda. He paid for the drinks and carried them outside near an unoccupied bench. The breeze helped the humidness of the hot night somewhat.

Gloria sipped her soda, trying not to think of the calories. She preferred diet cola, but it contained caffeine and she tried to stay away from that. "It's packed in here."

"Usual for a Friday night."

Gloria felt the solidness of Matt's body against hers. She wanted to lean closer. A man squeezed in between the people standing by her and pushed her into Matt.

"Sorry," Gloria mumbled and cringed as she almost spilled her soda on Matt.

"That's okay." Matt wrapped his arm around her.

Gloria's heart beat faster and she turned to look at Matt. She stared at his lips, then looked up into his dark brown eyes, so close, like looking at dark chocolate frosting. Gloria bit her lip.

"I think we should have stayed at my place." Matt tightened his arm around her.

Knowing that Matt felt the same attraction she did caused the quivering sensations throughout her body again. The noise of the restaurant diminished as she continued to stare into Matt's eyes. Unconsciously, her body began to inch closer to him.

"Matt, table for two!" The hostess shouted.

"Saved by the hostess?" Gloria asked.

"Damn!"

They followed her to a table in the center of the nautical themed restaurant. The tables were made of rough wood. On Gloria's first visit to the place she'd feared she'd jab her finger with a splinter, but found the table tops were smooth. On the brown walls hung pictures of sailing ships and pirate ships.

When the waitress came, Gloria ordered the grilled chicken Caesar salad. Salad was fairly easy to eat. Somehow, she felt that eating a sandwich would be awkward in front of Matt. She remembered the sandwiches were huge here.

Matt ordered fish and shrimp. "How come you don't like seafood?"

"I suppose because in my family we never ate it. We were more of a beef and potatoes kind of family. Ground beef, that is, and chicken on Sundays. Plus Mexican rice and pinto beans. I used to like tuna sandwiches, but I don't anymore."

"My family lived on fish during the summer. Dad used to go fishing at the coast, Port Aransas, about three hours south of here. He'd take us for a week, on vacation, then he went every other weekend and would always bring back fish. Mom would fry, bake, or broil it. Dad even barbecued it a few times.

"Barbecued?"

"Dad would do things like that. Drove my Mom crazy."

Gloria laughed. "Your dad sounds like an interesting person."

"He is." Matt's shoulders sagged.

"Is he sick?"

"No." He looked horrified at the thought, his eyes widened and she could have sworn he shuddered. "At least I don't think so. But he's getting older."

"I know. My Dad just turned seventy-five. I realized the other day that he's only got twenty-five more years to live, at most. How many people live beyond or up to one hundred years old? Twenty-five years seems like such a short time. Especially when it concerns a loved one."

"Yeah," Matt said quietly and turned away to sip his beer.

Gloria saw the waitress with the food. Sighing, she knew she had said too much. Why was she nervous? Because she had gone out with a man.

When the waitress left, Gloria apologized, "Sometimes, I say too much."

"Don't worry about it, Gloria."

"Anyway, my dad isn't letting age stop him. He's on a senior citizens' cruise to Cancun for a couple of weeks."

"Good for him," Matt said and picked up a piece of fried shrimp. "Ummm!"

The tantalizing smell of fish mixed with chicken wafted in the air. She picked up her knife and fork. The succulent spicy meat tasted tender and delicious.

"You said it."

"You want to taste?"

Gloria wrinkled her nose. "No, thanks."

Matt held the fried shrimp speared on his fork and waved it under her nose.

"I have tried it, believe me. I even tried a fried oyster once at the Oyster Bake at Saint Mary's University, you know, their annual fiesta?"

"Okay. But you're not a true San Antonian without liking fish from Moe's Seafood."

****

On the drive home, Gloria felt good. She had gone out to dinner with a good-looking man, and she had enjoyed herself. She thought he had, too. She held her leftover salad in a carton on her lap. She had been too nervous to eat much and had enjoyed their conversation a lot. She and Matt didn't seem to have the same likes and dislikes, at least not about food, but they both came from close families and that said a lot at her age—and his.

Matt parked in front of her house. "Thanks for going out with me."

"Thanks for asking."

"I'll be back Monday night. I'll call you tomorrow."

"You'll be busy." Gloria didn't want him to feel obligated.

"Not too busy to call you." Matt leaned towards her and kissed her lightly on the lips.

She edged closer to him on the seat. She heard something slide to the floor of the truck, but her senses were more tuned to the feel of Matt's lips on hers. She put her arms around his neck, he pulled her closer and she felt his warmth and the hardness of his body. The smell of his spicy cologne filled her nostrils. The sensation of his hair under her fingertips felt soft and rough at the same time.

He lifted his lips and stared into her eyes. "This is going to get out of hand real easy."

"I know." Gloria put her lips on his again. She felt his kiss from her lips to her core. She wanted him in her bed—or his—in the bed of the truck—on the lawn in front of her house. Anywhere! But—no! She hardly knew him. He hardly knew her. As she felt his hands on her body and his lips on hers, she wondered, what did that matter? But it did.

"Goodnight, Matt," she murmured against his mouth.

"You sure?" His hands caressed her back.

"Yes."

"Okay."

Matt walked her to the door and kissed her once more. She couldn't resist and gave herself up to his kiss, losing track of time.

"Mom!" Gordy had returned from the movies. Had Will seen her, too?

Gloria wrenched her lips from Matt's. Oh no! She should have just gone inside the house. What would Gordy think of her? Kissing a strange man in front of her house under the porch light no less.

"What are you doing?"

"Uh...Gordy, sweetie. This is Matt." Her hands flew to her hair to smooth it.

"I know. The yardman."

Matt held out his hand to her son. "Hi, Gordy."

Without another word or acknowledgement, Gordy unlocked the door and went in.

"I'm sorry. I guess I shouldn't have..."

"Gloria, you're a grown woman." Matt reminded her.

"I know, but...I haven't...you know." Gloria stopped

and took Matt's hand and shook it. "This is how we should have ended tonight. Actually, we shouldn't even have gone out."

"Why not? Didn't you have a good time?" Matt grinned.

"Yes, but..." Gloria shrugged. "Matt, my sons haven't seen me with another man for years. This isn't easy for them."

"Sounds as if it's not easy for you either." Matt kissed her lightly. "We ended the night almost right."

"What?"

"We should have stayed at my house and made love." Matt turned to go. "But we will eventually do that."

Chapter Four

"Tanya, it's good to hear from you." Gloria smiled, happy to hear her friend's voice on the phone. She put the book she'd been reading down on the coffee table.

"How're your roses?"

"Still wilting, but Matt sprayed them with fungicide and put down some fertilizer. He'll be back on Monday to check on them."

"Really? Well, you may not need to wait until Monday. Remember, I'm having the masquerade party tonight. We're going to dress up. Even though Wayne is throwing a fit. Why does he do that? He knows he's going to have to give in. So, are you coming? I'm inviting Matt, too."

"Oh, Tanya, I'm sorry I forgot. I haven't the foggiest idea what to wear." Gloria fidgeted with the book she held in her hand. "Besides..."

Nowadays, she never felt well. The new medicine made her feel nauseated and dizzy. And irritable. Her sons told her so. Lately, she snapped at them for the smallest thing. Like last night when Gordy got angry over finding her necking under a porch light. Not that it was a small thing. For either of them. As she had told Matt, a man hadn't been a part of her life for a long time. Her youngest son didn't even remember a time when his dad had lived with them. However, she shouldn't have scolded him so harshly last night. She sighed.

"What's the matter? Is something wrong between you and Matt? Because if there is, I'll set that man straight right away. I'm sure it's his fault. Or, maybe not. What did you do, Gloria?"

"Nothing," Gloria said. Tanya always jumped to conclusions. "It's just, well. I haven't been feeling very well lately."

"Are you pregnant?"

"Tanya! For goodness sake! I just met him yesterday

and my oldest son is twenty years old! I'm not even sure if I remember what to do with a baby." Gloria exclaimed and hoped Wayne wasn't within hearing range.

"Well, true, but still…"

"Maybe it's just allergies or lack of sleep."

"Now, we're getting somewhere." Tanya's laughter came over the phone line.

Gloria smiled in spite of herself. "What time will the party be?"

"Oh, people start trickling in about eight, but the party won't get started until nine. Wayne isn't barbecuing, though. We're having the party catered. He said he just wants to sit back and enjoy himself this time. As if he doesn't when he barbecues, talking and drinking with his buddies. However, I do want him to wear his costume, so I won't point that out to him—much. So Gloria, what's the real reason?"

"Real reason?" After Tanya's long answer to her question, Gloria had forgotten what her friend was talking about.

"For that whiny '*I don't feel well*' thing?"

"Health issues. I have some health issues." Gloria sighed again.

"Are you dying?"

"No, but…"

"No buts, *amiga*. Get your butt to my party. I'll see you at eight, or thereabouts."

Before she could protest, Tanya hung up the phone.

Gloria held the phone in her hand. She must call her doctor soon. She hated this feeling of anxiousness. Really, there was no reason for that. Not with so much in her life to be happy about. It was the damn medication, not her life, that was messing her up.

****

"Your roses are doing nicely." Matt hunched down in front of the rosebushes in her yard.

Gloria stood near him as he worked. He had surprised her by coming over unannounced. Her heart lifted at the sight of him.

"I'm so happy."

Matt stood, put his arm around her and kissed her lightly on the lips. "Glad I could help."

33

L. M. Gonzalez

"Yes, you did."

Matt unrolled the garden hose and watered the rosebushes. "Just a little sprinkle of water. We haven't had any rain lately. What are you doing today?"

"Tanya called. She's having a party."

"Yeah, she told me about it, too." Matt finished watering the roses. "Let's go to my place and decide whether we want to go to Tanya's, or just stay there."

Gloria's heart fluttered in her breast. *Just stay there.*

During the drive to Matt's house, Gloria wondered if she should tell Matt about her high blood pressure. It was no big deal. Besides, she was on meds. He always got so sad when he looked at her roses. She knew it wasn't because they were dying. Could roses and sickness be connected in his mind? And he had shuddered visibly at the thought of his dad getting sick. Of course, who wouldn't? Still...

Once at Matt's house, he got drinks and she tried not to think about her health issues.

"Do you want to go to Tanya and Wayne's party?" Matt joined her on the sofa. The TV was muted to a basketball game.

"If you do." Gloria moved a little to allow Matt more room. He reached out and kept her close.

"Yes or no, Gloria?"

"Maybe. If you do." She settled deeper into Matt's sofa and closed her eyes, feeling dizzy. Probably due to his nearness. his warm body against her back.

"Are you okay?" Matt asked, sounding concerned.

"I don't feel my best. Just a little dizzy." Gloria felt Matt's body stiffen. "What's the matter, Matt?"

"Uh, nothing."

She noticed his body didn't relax. Should she tell him about her high blood pressure? No, not yet. She'd wait until she saw the doctor again.

"Listen, we don't have to go to the party. I'll stay here with you and massage your feet, shoulders, back—whatever."

"Sounds nice."

"Don't want it to be nice. Turn around and let me see your feet."

Gloria turned even though it felt so good to be this

close to Matt. He took her shoes off and tossed them behind him. "I want you to feel woozy, as if you've just finished a margarita."

"I shouldn't drink anymore."

Matt began to massage her foot. She felt shivers throughout her body. Who knew her toes could be so sensitive? She sighed.

"Feel better?"

"Yes. They ought to bottle you." Gloria closed her eyes.

"Huh?"

"Never mind."

Matt pulled her close and kissed her. She loved to kiss this man. How many had it been so far? Who was counting anyway? She only felt. Felt his soft, firm mouth on hers, and a trembling, warm sensation that only Matt could evoke.

"Umm!"

"I agree." Matt said. "We stay here, then?"

"We can't let Tanya down. We have to dress up, though," Gloria murmured as she felt Matt's lips on her neck.

"As in suit and tie?" Matt sat up to continue his magic with her feet.

"As in mask and flowing robe, or something." Gloria still didn't open her eyes.

"I'll dress up as a gardener."

Gloria opened her eyes. "That's not fair. Besides, what could I be? We have to complement each other."

"A very pretty flower girl. A rose princess."

"Rose princess!" Gloria's heart skipped a beat. "Oh Matt, that's so sweet."

"I'm a lot of things, Gloria, but sweet isn't one of them."

"I beg to differ." Gloria threw a green sofa pillow at him.

"Okay! Okay!" Matt laughed.

Feeling mischievous, Gloria said, "I think I'll be 'Mary Mary Quite Contrary'."

"Who's that?"

"You know, from the nursery rhyme, I think she wore a blue dress and an apron. What color was the apron?

Probably white, right? I can also wear a hat and I'll carry a watering can."

"Very out of character. You don't water your garden." Matt held out his hands and shrugged.

"Only because I thought I was over-watering."

Matt grinned.

"Oh you! Make one mistake and I'm not allowed to forget it!" Gloria regretted throwing that sofa pillow at Matt before. Now, he really deserved it. She got up from the sofa and walked to the computer. "I'm going to look up 'Mary' to see how she dressed."

"So, I'm dressing up like a gardener?"

"If I can find out how Mary dresses." Gloria said and waited for the search engine to bring up possible websites. "Look!" She does wear blue. And a straw-looking hat. I can get one at the discount store. I bought one before, but returned it. I couldn't see myself wearing it." She read the narrative on the screen. "Oh no!"

"What now?"

"You know this nursery rhyme is pretty violent and I read this thing to my boys when they were little."

"What do you mean?"

"Mary is apparently 'Bloody Mary', an English queen, who killed and tortured anyone who didn't practice the Catholic faith. The *silver bells and cockleshells* may have been instruments of torture and the *pretty maids all in a row* refer to the guillotine. How awful."

"Forget about all that. All you wanted to know was how she dressed. Now you do."

"You know there's a list here of other nursery rhymes. All of them probably have a violent meaning as well."

"Gloria, come over here. It may not even be true. You can't always trust what's on the web."

"I know, but I'm very disappointed, though." Gloria sat down on the sofa again.

Matt gathered her close in his arms and said, "That's what I like about you. You care so much."

"Oh yeah?"

"Yeah."

She nuzzled his neck. "This is getting somewhere fast."

"Let's go there—fast." Matt nuzzled her ear.

His warm breath tickled her, but she also felt a shivering that had nothing to do with cold.

After long minutes of kissing, Matt said, "I hate to say this, but I have to take you back. My helper is waiting."

Gloria held on to him. "Leave him there."

"I wish I could. I'll see you tonight, okay? We can end the evening right this time."

Gloria's stomach did flip flops. Was she ready for this? Was this the right time? Her feelings for Matt were becoming stronger with each passing moment.

Once home, the feeling of anxiousness crept up on Gloria again. She hated this. What was wrong with her? Maybe it was tension. The doctor suggested she lose weight. She knew what she had to do. Exercise was a good way to relieve stress. Changing her clothes to sweats, she jogged out to the shed where she and her sons had set up the treadmill and the exercise bicycle. Since the shed featured no windows, she had hung landscape scenes on all four sides. The pictures were a place for her to look when she felt like giving up. The music on her CD player helped as well. Every day she walked the treadmill for twenty minutes, then rode the bicycle for another twenty. A little high blood pressure was not going to conquer her. She needed to feel her best for tonight. Her stomach turned over again. She wouldn't think about it. Gloria decided to see how it all played out, to use the phrase her sons did. Still, her heart fluttered wildly as she walked the treadmill and it wasn't all due to exercise.

****

"Hi! My favorite gardener is here!" Tanya, dressed as a cheerleader in a red uniform, ran toward Matt and grabbed his face and kissed him squarely on the mouth. "Hi, gorgeous!"

"Hey, don't go around kissing other gardeners, Tanya." Wayne, complementing his wife, dressed as a football player. He walked up with two beers in his hands. Matt looked as he had earlier today in her garden—in jeans, work shirt and cap, plus those muscles.

Gloria, for her part, almost wanted to slap Tanya for grabbing Matt. Why? She hadn't thought she was a jealous person. Besides, Tanya was her friend. She took the beer from Wayne, but wanted something else to drink, preferably, non-alcoholic.

Matt grinned and pushed Tanya gently away and took the beer from Wayne.

"How're the roses doing?" Wayne asked. "Hey, you look like a little gardener yourself."

"Still alive." Gloria said, shaking off her feeling of jealousy. "I'm 'Mary Mary Quite Contrary'."

"The nursery rhyme?"

Matt laughed. "Please don't get her started on nursery rhymes."

"Huh? Well, Matt knows his roses. Not me. At least not as well. Come outside." Wayne invited Matt.

"That man!" Tanya's blond ponytail flipped up as she turned to look at Gloria. Her friend always experimented with hair color. "He thinks I don't know what he's doing out there. I tell him to quit smoking and he won't listen to me. Keeps on smoking like a train."

"Do you need help with anything?" Gloria asked, silently berating herself for her jealous thoughts earlier. Tanya's interest rested on only one man and that man was her husband.

"Well, maybe. Come to the kitchen with me and I'll see what's going on. It's still early. Hey, I like your costume. Very original. Do you like my blond hair?"

Before Gloria could respond, Tanya continued, "This is my sister, Molly and her husband." She pointed to a couple dressed as a king and queen. Gloria didn't know her history that well to know which king and queen. Next, Tanya pointed to a burger, fries and Coke. "That's Peter, Sebastian and Pearl, friends of theirs. You guys are making me hungry."

Gloria smiled at them and their costumes. Friendly laughter echoed in Gloria's ears as she followed Tanya into the kitchen.

A group of ladies in brown uniforms and name tags were filling bowls of chips and platters of dip with more chips to take into the living room. "The catering crew." Tanya said, as the group left the kitchen.

Gloria set the beer down on the counter and asked, "Do you have a soda, Tanya?"

"Sure thing." Tanya handed her one. "Looks like they've got everything taken care of. Let's go into the living room. Change that god-awful metal rock Wayne has on out there. Put on some country-western. Or, do you want Tejano?"

"Whatever you want, Tanya. By the way, where are your kids?"

Tanya's daughter was fifteen, her son, eighteen.

"Out with friends. Junior drove. Even though he's a good driver, I always worry about him. Nikki is out to the movies. Carol's mom drove them and will pick them up. I worry about her because there's so much kids can get into nowadays."

Gloria nodded her agreement.

Tanya busied herself with greeting more guests. Gloria sipped her soda and looked for Matt. She saw him by the door.

"Did you miss me?" Matt asked.

"Horribly."

Soft music filled the room. "Let's dance." Matt led her to the middle of the living room where Tanya had cleared the space for dancing by pushing light-colored floral print sofas against the walls. Dim lighting with small lamps and votive candles made the room intimate.

"Okay." Gloria walked into Matt's arms. As she put her arms around Matt's neck and inched close to his body, she remembered his words. Tonight, the evening would have a different ending. She shivered with anticipation. When she was in his arms, she felt that she was ready for anything, but when she was by herself, her fears returned. It had been so long.

Matt nuzzled her neck. She sighed. Yes, it had seemed like forever since she had been with a man.

When the dance ended, Tanya announced it was time to eat.

"We're going on a cruise to Europe next month." Tanya supervised the serving of the food—brisket, sausage, chicken along with potato salad, pinto beans and bread. For dessert, peach cobbler. Gloria's mouth watered at the thought, but knew she had to pass it up.

"I thought you said you and Wayne were staying home this year." Gloria reminded her friend.

"I couldn't pass this cruise up. It's a steal. For three grand, we'll get to see London, Paris, Rome, and Greece. Can you imagine? I've always wanted to go there, ever since I graduated from high school. I planned it all out. I would work all summer and earn the money to go, but then I met Wayne and well, you know, as they say, the rest is history. Though I wouldn't give Wayne up for the world. Still, I can't help wishing that he hadn't come into my life so soon. But now, my dream can come true. I'm going to Europe!"

"I'm so happy for you, Tanya. How does Wayne feel about it?" Gloria held out her plate to be filled with food. Throwing caution to the wind, she got a little bit of brisket, even though her stomach was churning at the thought of Matt and later in the evening at his house. She wasn't sure she could eat.

"Oh Wayne! He'll do anything I say." Tanya looked at Wayne talking to a *billboard*. "Who is that man talking to?"

"Hi, Tanya! It's Talia. Remember me?" The *billboard* waved with both hands.

"Damn bimbo. Who invited her?"

"You?"

"Never. She's always hanging around Wayne. Oh, she came with Bob. Poor Bob. He's fixing to get his sweet heart broken. That bimbo is murder on nice guys." Tanya waved back.

Gloria laughed and joined Matt at a table. Tanya had set up several small tables for four around the huge dining room. She had decorated them with white tablecloths and yellow and orange mums.

"What took you so long?" Matt bit into a chicken leg.

"Tanya told me she and Wayne are going on a European cruise."

"Yeah, Wayne told me about it, too. Have you ever been on a cruise?"

Gloria picked at her potato salad. "No."

"Do you want to?"

Gloria looked up at Matt. What had he asked her? Did she want to what? Have a relationship? Make love? She wasn't sure. Yet, she was.

"What?" She pushed her mound of potato salad

almost off the plate.

"Am I pushing you too hard?" Matt picked up his glass of water.

Gloria didn't pretend not to know what Matt was asking her. "Maybe. I'm so mixed up."

"I'm not going to force you into anything, 'Mary, Mary'," Matt grinned.

Gloria smiled. "I'm sorry. I feel like a teenager, emotionally, you know? I mean, it's been a long time. I don't want to make a mistake."

"Look, let's just enjoy the party. And, if anything more happens, it happens. If it doesn't, it doesn't."

Gloria grabbed his hand and when she felt the warmth, the calluses, the strength, she felt as if she could go anywhere with this man. Maybe she was overanalyzing. Love didn't call for analysis, but for feelings. She was going to go with her feelings tonight. "Thank you."

"Let's dance some more. I like you in my arms." Matt offered his hand to her.

"I like that, too."

Gloria danced with Matt until he suggested they go outside. The moonlit night was hot and humid, as summer nights were in San Antonio, but with Matt so near to her, she didn't care.

"I guess we can't cool off in this heat."

"The stars are out tonight. Usually I can't see them. Or maybe it's that I seldom go outside." Gloria pointed up to the night sky.

"Yes, they are out. And so are we." Matt took her in his arms.

His mouth covered hers. At first, she was afraid someone would come out and see them. As Matt continued his sweet assault on her mouth, she forgot everything except the man in her arms. She felt his hands caress her back down to her hips as he pulled her nearer to him. She straddled his leg.

"Take off that apron. We can use it as our bed of love," Matt gasped against her mouth.

Gloria giggled. "We can't use *Mary, Mary's apron*."

"Let's get out of here then."

While Matt thanked Wayne for the party, Gloria

went to say good-bye to Tanya, who was in the middle of a bingo game. "What? Leaving already? The party's barely starting," Tanya grinned. "Oh, I know! You want to go have your own party."

Gloria cringed, no one at this party knew her, but did Tanya have to announce it to everyone?

"Thanks for coming, Gloria. Enjoy the rest of the night." Tanya smacked her on the behind.

"That Tanya," Gloria said, as she and Matt walked to his truck.

"I don't care who knows." Matt grabbed her and pulled her inside the truck.

His kisses filled her senses. Her arms wrapped around him. His hand lifted her blue dress and apron and inched up her leg. Delicious shivers ran up and down her spine. He kept kissing her and the truck seat wasn't big enough for her to feel the entire length of his body on hers, and she wanted that. She was about to tell Matt to take her to his house. She was ready. Now! But then, visions of her sons intruded. No, she couldn't do this. It was too late. Her time had passed. She was a mother. She was in her forties, for God's sake.

"Matt, please stop."

"Gloria?" Matt's voice sounded far away.

"Not tonight, Matt. I can't. Take me home."

Matt straightened up in his seat. "Why, Gloria?"

"It's too late for me. I can't." She took off her hat, which had fallen off her head, the ribbon was choking her.

"What do you mean too late? You're not making sense."

"I know." Gloria placed the ribbon inside the hat.

Matt turned the key in the ignition. "Forget it. I don't want to know why. It's your decision."

As Matt drove her home, she tried to explain what she meant, but he didn't want to hear. She wasn't sure how to explain anyway. At her house, he walked her to the door, but only made sure she unlocked it, then he left without kissing her.

"Matt?"

"Goodnight, Gloria."

Chapter Five

"Gordo is going on a date," Dex announced from the computer area where he sat.

"What?" Gloria looked at her youngest son sitting in the living room. She had just cut some roses from her garden, happy to see they hadn't gotten any worse, and was arranging them in a vase at the dining table. The fungicide and fertilizer were working.

"Oh, man! Why did you tell Mom?" Gordy squirmed in the armchair.

"Why didn't you want me to know, Gordy?" Gloria asked, hurt.

"It's no big deal."

"I think it is. You've never had an official date. Is this an official date?"

"I guess so," Her son said, not looking at her.

"Did you meet her at school?"

"No."

Gordy wasn't the type who would openly divulge information, she must ask questions. She'd learned that about him from the time he first got into trouble in school when he was little. "Where did you meet her?"

He avoided his mom's eyes and almost looked as if he wouldn't answer by the frown on his face. "Last time I went to the movies with Will. His girlfriend brought some girls along. This one attached herself to me."

"Sounds like you didn't like her." Gloria looked at her arrangement of flowers.

"Not at that time."

"What changed?" Gloria turned her attention to her youngest son.

"Will's girlfriend has restrictions."

"What do you mean?" Gloria sat on the arm of the sofa.

Gordy shrugged. "Her mom doesn't want her to go out with Will alone for awhile."

"What happened? Did things get out of control?"

Gordy squirmed again in the armchair. "I don't know, Mom. I don't ask."

"Do you want to go out with this girl? Or is it just a favor for Will?"

"I wouldn't go out with a girl for Will."

"I hope not. But then, going out with a girl because you like her is even scarier."

"What?" Gordy stared at his mom with a question in his eyes.

"That's how Moms talk, Gordo." Dex said, not looking up from the computer.

"Do you know who this girl is, Dex?"

"No. I haven't met her."

"I'm not bringing her to '*meet the parents*'," Gordy said with an angry gleam in his eye.

"Of course not. You only have to introduce her to your Mom and your brother."

"Not this time." Gordy shook his head.

At Gloria's frown, he continued, "I'm driving to Will's. From there, we'll go pick them up in Will's car."

"Both of them will be at Will's girlfriends' house?"

"Yeah."

Gloria was still in two minds about this, but her son was going to be a senior in high school. She had to loosen the reins a little. Still...

"I hope you have a good time, Gordy." Gloria grinned, remembering this was her youngest son and he was going on his first date.

"Aw, Mom!" Gordy looked as if he knew what was coming.

"It's so sweet, *mijo*. Your first date." She used the endearment which meant *my son*.

"Don't make me sound like some lame duck who's never known any girls." Gordy walked toward his room.

"Oh, I know. You did have a *spot* with a girl in eighth grade, didn't you?" Gloria teased him.

"Yeah, wuss, remember your spot?" Dex laughed.

Gordy stopped to punch his brother in the stomach.

Gloria said, "I won't tease anymore, Gordy. I'll control myself."

"Man! Am I glad I'm not bringing her over here!"

"Gordy, really! I wouldn't embarrass you. Did I ever do that with you, Dex?"

"She didn't, fool. Don't worry so much." Dex looked up from the computer screen this time.

"What am I going to wear?" Walking to his room, he put his hands on his head. "I've gotta work on my hair, too!"

"Well, that puts aside the theory that men don't agonize about what to wear and how their hair looks," Gloria said.

Dex followed him to their room, laughing and teasing his little brother. He had no qualms about continuing the ribbing.

As she watched her sons leave the room, Gloria didn't know what to think.

Just the other night, she had asked Gordy if he had a girlfriend. Grinning at her, he asked if she wanted him to have a girlfriend. Smiling back, Gloria told him she just wondered. She wasn't in any hurry for him to have one if he wasn't.

Gloria knew that would bring a whole new set of challenges. She and Dex had their first bad argument when he was sixteen over his first girlfriend. They were on the phone constantly and Gloria had wanted to set a time limit. Dex had protested, refused to do it and, thus, their first argument. They'd seemed to fall in love so quickly; planned to get married, would fall asleep talking to each other on the phone. And when his heart broke several months later, she cried inside for him. First love was always so precious, but so fleeting as well at times. And it hurt so much to lose it.

Maybe that's why Gloria had never fallen in love before. *Before what, Gloria?* She wasn't in love now. She was just having a good time with Matt. But love? Since her divorce, she had dated a few times, but most of the time she had been so busy raising the boys that she had no time for men, especially for nurturing a relationship. As she had gotten older, she had also grown in wisdom. A woman didn't just fall in love with the man. She had his personality to deal with, his baggage, his quirks and oh God, yes, his family. As a single woman, she might be more ready to accommodate, but not as a forty-something woman with two grown sons. Until now.

No, not yet. Not now. Matt might be a nice man, very attractive, a great kisser, such wonderful hands. But...he had baggage, an ex-wife, three daughters and seven siblings. Besides, she had high blood pressure and issues with her meds. What if she had a stroke? She worried about that even though with medicine, her blood pressure remained normal. She continued her exercise routine and watched what she ate because she didn't want to take meds forever.

She hadn't told Matt about her health issues. She didn't want to. Did he have to know? They weren't officially dating. They weren't committed to each other. Besides, how would her boys feel about Matt? How would his daughters feel about her? These were things that had stopped her the other night. And now Matt hadn't called her.

****

"Matt, you need to start paying alimony to me again." His ex-wife's voice grated through the cell phone.

"What? Angela, you're kidding, right?"

"That creep, Jorge, left me. Packed his bags and left. *Pinche viejo*! I know he found someone else."

Matt kept his mouth shut, but the thought of asking her how it felt to be betrayed was on the tip of his tongue. "So, the bozo left you and you want money from me? You've got some nerve, woman."

"What's the matter? You can't afford it anymore? The girls told me you're going out with some goddamn bimbo."

"We're not talking about that, Angela," Matt said and threw his working gloves on the front seat of the truck. She had called him in the middle of a job. His new worker hadn't shown up and he hadn't had time to hire another one. Today was Sunday, too.

"Okay, we won't. But, I need money. Or, I'll take my cut from the child support."

"Angela, do that and I'll take you to court for full custody."

"You wouldn't win. I'm a good mother in spite of what you think. No court in the country would take my girls from me."

Matt hated to admit it, but Angela was right. Even if

46

she took money from the girls' child support, she would see to it that they had everything they needed.

"Why don't you come over and we'll talk about it. I need to buy a certain something. Help me with that and I won't bother you again about money. I'm looking into getting a job."

"You, a job, Angela?" Matt looked up at the sky. "Please, don't make it rain today. I've got a lot of work to do."

"What are you talking about, Matt? You're not listening to me, are you? That's it, isn't it?"

"Angela. I'll be over tonight after my last job."

"I'll meet you at your house. Amber invited some of her friends over. They'll be in and out of the kitchen and living room all evening. We won't have any privacy. Unless we meet in our bedroom?"

"Not on your life. Not after that man has been in it."

"How boring you are." Angela's voice drawled out.

"Lucky for me. Not everyone thinks that way."

Matt closed his cell with a snap. Just what he needed. To have his ex-wife visit on the weekend. He needed to talk to Gloria. What happened? He knew he should have handled the situation better. Women! That's why he liked plants and flowers, even weeds. With a hack here and a spray of fungicide there, the problem was gone.

****

"Oh, Matt! I still miss you so much!" Angela threw herself in his arms and kissed him, full on the lips. Even though she had a petite frame, she almost knocked him off his feet. He pushed her away, none too gently. He noticed that her normally long black hair was red today.

"Angela, come on. Tell me what your problem is." As usual, she wore too much perfume. Matt stopped himself from commenting on it.

"It's not a problem, darling. I just need some money."

"Which you don't have. I'd call that a problem." Matt walked toward the kitchen.

"You're so logical. That's what I always hated about you."

"Do you want a drink?" He opened the refrigerator door.

"Of course. A margarita." Angela climbed up on a

stool in front of the counter.

"This isn't a bar, Angela. Besides, all I have is juice and soda."

"A soda, then."

Matt opened the refrigerator, grabbed two cans of grape soda and handed her one.

"What do you want to buy?" Matt looked at the clock.

"Are you going to time me? Or do you have a date?"

"Neither. Just start talking."

"I want to buy a kit. It costs $499," Angela stated and took a long sip of her drink.

"What is it? A selling job?"

"No, it's a kit that includes books, CDs, workbooks. I think it has something to do with stocks."

"You think? You're not getting involved with something you know nothing about and endanger the girls' futures."

"I would never do that, Matt, and you know it." Angela slid the can of soda from one hand to the other.

"I'm not so sure about you anymore, especially since that bozo."

"Don't talk to me about that creep." Angela's thick brows came together and her enormous eyes blazed anger.

"Look into something else to make money. This stock kit sounds too iffy." Matt finished his soda and threw the can in the trash.

"Why don't you like to take risks?" Angela whined.

"I take them every day."

"Oh yeah. A gardener's job is risky. The lawn mower might turn around and bite you," Angela smirked.

"I know you've never had any respect for what I do, but it pays the bills." Matt crossed his arms on his chest.

"Yes, and that's about all it ever did." She took a sip of soda. "When I think of all those men I turned down. You remember Carl Lujan? He's in New York, on Wall Street, making a million dollars, more probably. I saw him and his wife at the last high school reunion. You didn't go."

"Why would I want to go see a bunch of people I wasn't comfortable with then, and for sure not now?" Matt got up to get a dishrag to wipe down the counter.

"You're so boring." Angela fluffed her hair.

"Say that one more time and I'll show you how boring I really can be."

"Actually, you are not boring. You never were." Angela said and inched around the counter closer to Matt.

"Hey, wait a minute." Matt dropped the dishrag and put his hands up to ward Angela off.

"I can make you remember the exciting times we had."

"Angela…"

Before he could prevent it, her arms crept around his neck and she kissed him.

"Excuse me, the door was unlocked. I thought I'd surprise you."

Gloria! Matt pushed Angela away. He saw his ex-wife grin and straighten her hair.

"I'm the one surprised," Gloria ran.

"Gloria, wait!"

Matt heard Angela's laughter as he ran after Gloria.
****

Gloria ran to her car. Stupid! She had been so stupid not to call before she came. Matt wasn't committed to her. How could she have just barged in like that? About to open the car door, she heard Matt calling her.

"Gloria, please wait!"

"I'm sorry I came over unannounced. I should have called, especially after last night."

"Why should you have called? You don't need an invitation." Matt ran his fingers through his hair, messing it up. "That's my ex-wife, Angela."

Gloria adjusted the purse strap on her shoulder, but didn't speak. His ex-wife, Angela, long reddish-brown hair and thin body. Julia looked like her mother.

"She came over to borrow some money. Broke up with her boyfriend and I guess…" Matt stopped talking.

Gloria shrugged. "I have no hold on you, Matt. You don't owe me any explanations."

"Matt, darling. I'm not through with you yet." Angela said in a sing-song voice.

"I'll get rid of her and we can spend some time together."

"Not tonight, Matt." Gloria opened the car door and pushed back the hair from her face. The heat seemed to engulf her in waves. Cicadas buzzed in the trees. The whoosh of the cars on the nearby freeway seemed far away. As far away as Matt seemed to be from her.

"I'll call you tomorrow. I want to apologize..."

She closed the door on anything else he might have wanted to say.

Gloria watched him through the rear view mirror, and saw Angela run out, throwing her arms around him.

Fool! She was a damn fool. He had walked away from her last night. How could she have thought she could come tonight and they could pick up where they left off? Too late again. It was just too late for her.

****

Monday morning, Gloria resented having to go to work. How was she going to make it through the day? She couldn't stop thinking about Matt with his ex-wife.

Her friend and co-worker leaned her round figure against the door frame of Gloria's office.

"Glad you're back," Beatrice Lopez said. She had been at Home Nursing as long as Gloria had, doing insurance claims billing. "How are your roses?"

"I think they'll be fine." She tried to smile. Should she tell Beatrice about Matt? Before she could make up her mind, her friend continued.

"Look at my hair. I went to get a perm and the stylist messed up. It's standing on end." Beatrice pointed to her dark brown hair.

"I did notice it looked a bit frizzy," Gloria grinned.

"I almost didn't pay the woman. Told her I was never going back there again." Without waiting for a response, she said, "I got my girls registered at school. I'm off next week while I get them situated. Getting clothes and school supplies. Cindy is starting Kinder."

"I know that can be traumatic—more for the mom, than the child." Gloria said. This always happened. Beatrice would ask her about her weekend and soon she was talking about hers.

"Anything happen while I was gone?" she asked when she could get in a word.

"The usual. Nurses not turning in their paperwork until the last minute when it's payroll..."

She tuned Beatrice out. Maybe she should have

stayed home today.

"And we're having a lunch meeting today at 12:30 p.m. The boss has an announcement."

Gloria heard that. "What?"

"A meeting. I'm not sure what it's about. You know they never tell us anything until the last minute."

Once Beatrice went back to her office, Gloria checked her e-mail. There were a couple of updates from the regulating agency which oversaw Home Nursing. Nothing too drastic, thank goodness. She wasn't in the mood to draft new policies today,

Her phone rang and she picked it up.

"Gloria, can you come to my office?" Her boss, Liz, asked.

What did she want?

Gloria ambled to Beatrice's office. "Liz just called me into her office."

Beatrice shrugged. "Don't know what it could be about. Let me know if you find out anything. Friday, they were all behind closed doors as I told you."

Oops. Gloria had missed that part of Beatrice's monologue a minute ago.

"Close the door." Liz, dressed in a shiny sweat shirt, told her as Gloria arrived. Liz Canales was a tall woman, who tended to scare people because she rarely smiled. However, Gloria had known her for a long time and knew that was because Liz was basically a shy person. Something that had amazed Gloria since her boss had made a name for herself in the home health care business.

Gloria perched on the edge of a cushioned chair in front of Liz's L-shaped desk, which was covered with magazines, letters and reports. Behind the desk, her boss had a hutch, which was also covered with books and policy manuals.

"I have bad news, Gloria." Liz placed both hands on her desk calendar.

"For me?" Her stomach fluttered.

"For the company in general. We're in trouble." Liz sat back in her black executive chair.

"What do you mean?"

"You know we've been hearing about this reimbursement for improvements business, right?"

Gloria nodded. For months now, she had seen countless letters and e-mails regarding the new way that Kedco, a government payer, would pay their providers, of which Home Nursing was one. For years, Liz had tried to augment their referral base of primarily Kedco patients to include other payers, like private insurance. However, filling out the paperwork had proven to be a long and exhausting process. Most private insurances were preferred providers and agencies that were not on their list did not receive patient referrals.

"Kedco will pay agencies according to how well our outcomes improve. Like what percentage of our patients go into the hospital and whether or not they progress in activities of daily living, like dressing and going to the bathroom. In their wisdom, they've decided to pick a few agencies for a pilot project and we're one of the lucky ones who were chosen."

"What does that mean exactly?"

"As of next month, they're going to start paying us according to our improvement stats."

"Is that fair?"

"When has how we get paid been fair? We get what we get in this business." Liz picked up some papers. "Look at this desk. I need to clean this up. I can't work like this."

"So, Liz, what does this new paying system mean for the employees? For me?"

"Gloria, you've been with me for a long time. What is it now? Ten years?"

Gloria nodded.

"But I've gotta do what I've gotta do. I'm a business woman first and it might mean cutting down on staff." Liz picked up a stack of magazines and threw them in the trash.

"Is my job in danger?" Gloria's stomach sank. How would she provide for her family?

"All of our jobs are in danger. I'm going to notify the staff of this today, but I wanted to let you in on what was going on. We talked about this on Friday when you were gone. I almost called you, but I decided the bad news could wait. I didn't want to ruin your weekend. How was it, by the way?"

"Good." Gloria thought about Matt and smiled. Yes,

Liz had made a wise decision. Her weekend had started out fabulous. But now, she wasn't sure about Matt or her job.

"We'll make it through this one, too. We made it through the nineties with the Budget Act." Liz comforted.

"Just barely." Gloria shuddered at the thought.

****

"Dr. DeLeon, what is the matter with me?" Gloria had taken her lunch hour to go see her doctor.

"Anxious and dizzy, you said, right?" Dr. DeLeon put a pudgy finger up to his lips and tapped them. "It's the medication. I'm going to prescribe a lower dosage. Come back in six weeks. I'm also going to schedule you for an EKG."

"What's that? I mean I've heard about it. Some kind of heart monitoring, isn't it?"

Dr. DeLeon sat down on the stool. "An EKG is an electrocardiogram and it measures the electrical activity of the heartbeat. With each beat, an electrical impulse travels through the heart which causes the muscle to squeeze and pump blood from the heart. It measures if the electrical activity is normal or slow, fast or irregular. Also, I can find out whether your heart is enlarged or overworked."

"I don't think I want to find out."

"It'll be fine, Gloria. Just a precaution. Another test we could do is an echocardiogram. That's like a sonogram of your heart. I'll be able to see the strength of your heart muscle and if there's any valve damage."

"Goodness! Valve damage? Sounds like a problem with a car."

Dr. DeLeon made some quick notes, in her chart and smiled. "Sorry about that. However, I think it's just a matter of adjusting your medication. Don't stop taking it, though, even if you feel bad. That's one of the reasons a lot of people stop taking their BP meds. They don't quite feel right. It means the medication is working."

"I hate not feeling my best."

"I understand. Give it some time. Try to lose some more weight. That'll make you feel better."

Gloria thanked her doctor and left after paying at the cashier's desk. As she walked to her car, she thought of the two tests the doctor had mentioned. EKG? Echocardiogram? Did she really need such tests? Well, she had made an appointment for the EKG. She could only hope that whatever it showed would be normal.

Chapter Six

"Dad, something's the matter with Amber." Matt's oldest daughter, Julia said, as she walked into the kitchen where Matt was cooking, or attempting to.

"What?"

"She won't tell me. Says I won't understand since nothing ever bothers me. If you ask me, she's just a whiny baby."

"Did you tell her that?" Matt asked without looking up. He had his daughters for the weekend and lunch was fast becoming an ordeal. Patsy and Amber stated they wanted lasagna. So, here he was boiling noodles.

"Give me some credit."

Matt turned to look at his daughter, so much like Angela with her huge eyes. Thoughts of Angela also reminded him of last weekend with Gloria. He saw Julia wore a glittery short skirt over black tights that had no feet. What were those things called? Well, at least her legs were covered. He made no comment on her outfit, however. Numerous arguments had ensued over her choice of clothing. His comeback, that he knew how boys were, made no difference to his teenaged daughter intent on following the current fad.

"Uh, Dad. I don't think you were supposed to boil that. It's oven-ready lasagna."

"Shit."

"Dad." Julia mocked him. "Such language!"

Matt turned off the lasagna and proceeded to ladle it out of the pot onto the baking dish.

"We should have just ordered pizza." Julia watched her dad work.

"Next time we will."

Matt finished layering the lasagna, meat and cheese with Julia throwing in her two-cents as she saw fit. Covering the baking dish with foil, he placed it in the oven.

55

"There!"

"Did you turn the oven on, Dad?"

Matt gave her a look that asked who did she think she was talking to? He hadn't. "Thanks, honey." He walked toward her and kissed her cheek. "So, what's up with your sister?"

"She's a whiny baby."

"I am not! Daddy, tell her to stop calling me names!" Amber shouted.

Matt liked what his younger daughters wore—jeans and T-shirts, not revealing at all. "Girls, come on. Let's watch that movie, huh?" He led his daughters to the living room.

He had rented some movies, mostly romantic comedies; they had agreed to watch one action flick with him, but that would be the last one. That way if they lost interest he could enjoy it by himself.

Matt put the first DVD on.

"Daddy, can I talk to you?" Amber asked.

"We're going to watch a movie, baby." Matt told his daughter, as he was about to sit down.

"Please. And I'm not a baby. I wish everyone would remember that."

"So, stop acting like one." Patsy said and threw a green sofa pillow at her sister.

"Daddy!" Amber yelled.

"Be quiet. The movie is starting." Julia said and glared at both her younger sisters.

"Come to the kitchen, baby. We'll talk there." Matt led his youngest daughter away.

He poured some soda in glasses for both of them and sat at the table. Amber remained standing. Raising both thin arms, his daughter secured her ponytail with what looked like a rag to him and adjusted her glasses.

Heaving a big sigh, she spoke. "Daddy, I'm scared."

"Of what?" Matt's mind filled with visions of some boy harassing his baby girl, but he forced himself to remain quiet. Sometimes, his girls exaggerated.

"Of...of...oh, Daddy!" Amber burst into tears, collapsed on a nearby chair and buried her face in her hands, her ponytail flipping up over her head.

Matt flew to his daughter and knelt beside her.

"Amber, baby, what's the matter? What are you afraid of?"

"Oh, Daddy, I can't tell you! I thought I could, but it's a girl thing." She sobbed.

Matt felt as if his heart was in his throat. Was his baby pregnant? But she still watched cartoons. Matt refused to acknowledge that even at his age he watched cartoons and not watching them didn't necessarily mean a sign of maturity. Was she sick again? He refused to think about that.

"Have you talked to your mother about this?"

"She laughed at me. She said I was being ridiculous."

Matt decided he'd have a few choice words to say to Angela on Sunday evening when he took the girls back. How could she laugh at her daughter's problem?

"Are you sure you can't tell me?"

"No!" Amber wailed and ran back to the living room.

Not knowing what else to do, Matt joined his daughters. He heard Julia order her younger sister to be quiet. For a few long minutes, he watched Amber more than the movie. The oven timer went off and he hurried to the kitchen to take the lasagna out, remove the foil and bake it for another fifteen minutes per the directions on the box. After that, Matt left it on top of the stove with the oven temperature on warm until the movie ended.

The lasagna was a soggy mess. Putting the noodles to boil first had been a huge mistake. He tasted it. The meat and cheese were good at least. "Girls, come and eat. Sorry about the lasagna. Doesn't look too good."

"We're hungry, Daddy. We'll eat anything right now." Amber said with a smile. Apparently, she was over her crisis.

Girls! He'd never understand them. He noticed Julia ate more of her salad than the lasagna, though.

"I like this, Daddy. When Mom makes lasagna, it's hard around the edges." Patsy said.

How was Patsy doing? She was the least expressive of his daughters, the middle child, neither the oldest or the youngest. She would tell him if she had problems, right?

"Patsy, everything okay with you?"

"Sure, Dad."

"With your classes?"

"Yes." Patsy stared at him, frowning.

"Any trouble with boys?" Matt persisted.

Julia laughed. "Why would she have trouble? Boys don't notice her!"

Patsy hit Julia on the upper arm with her fist.

"Ow!" Julia yelled and massaged her arm. "Dad, did you see what she did?"

"She's mean! Just because I don't have a bunch of losers following me around."

"Not even one." Julia mocked.

"Not at the table, girls." Matt said. Maybe Patsy did have a few problems. She was too young for boys in her life anyway. Better they stayed away from her for another ten years.

****

The movie watching went well, Matt told himself as he put the DVD's away. The action flick was okay, but not the best. Maybe, he was just tired. He looked forward to spending time with his daughters, but he felt at a loss on how to deal with them sometimes. They had opted to miss the last movie which had been fine with him. He could still hear his daughters talking in their room.

Matt looked at the clock on the cable box—midnight. Should he call Gloria? Before he could change his mind, he picked up the phone and dialed her number.

"Gloria," Matt smiled. "Nice to hear your voice."

Silence greeted his words.

He pressed on. "I didn't call before because my daughters are here for the weekend."

"How's it going?" He heard her clear her throat.

"Well, I think, for the most part. Though Amber has a problem she can't tell me about. Any idea what it could be?"

"With a twelve-year-old girl it could be anything. Let me think back, back, back to when I was twelve."

Matt liked the sound of her voice in his ear, soothing yet sexy. "You don't have to go that far back."

"Since I raised two boys, I tend to forget what it was like being a girl. I've had to change my way of thinking to understand them." Her sigh came over the phone.

"I can relate. Sometimes, I feel I'm no help to my

girls." He placed the DVDs on the kitchen counter so he wouldn't forget to return them.

"Just being there for them helps, Matt, believe me."

"I wish I knew what's bothering Amber."

"She'll tell you eventually. Or, maybe her mother can help."

"I asked Amber about that. Angela didn't understand." Matt turned off the T.V. He stopped himself from berating Angela's reaction. Then, a terrible thought occurred. "Do you think she could be sick?"

"Surely, her mother would understand about that, wouldn't she?"

"Sure." Matt paused. "I hate sickness." Matt knew he sounded insane, but he couldn't help himself.

"Who doesn't? Especially when it concerns our kids." Gloria's soft voice transmitted total comprehension over the phone line.

"I know, but..." He persisted.

"It's probably just a girl thing."

"That's what she said," Matt harrumphed. "What is that exactly? 'A girl thing'? I don't get it."

"Of course you don't. You're not a girl." He heard Gloria's tinkling laugh in his ear and wished she were with him. "Ummm. What could it be?" Gloria was quiet for awhile.

"Gloria, you don't have to solve it right now."

"Oh. Right."

"Or, at all. It's my problem—and Amber's."

"Okay. Well... Enjoy the rest of your time with them."

"I will." Matt picked up a sofa pillow. "About the other night, Gloria. You do believe me about Angela, right?"

"Of course."

"I loaned her some money. That's all. I don't know what else she was up to, but I'm not interested."

Silence greeted his words a second time.

"Listen, maybe the next weekend I have the girls over we can all get together. What do you think?" Matt picked up a green sofa pillow from the floor and began tossing it up and down.

Gloria cleared her throat again. "Do you think that's a good idea?"

"I think so. Unless..." Matt paused and sat on the brown leather sofa.

"Unless what?"

"Unless you don't want to for some reason."

"What's going on between us, Matt? Is it just a temporary thing with you and me? If it is, then getting together with our kids is not a good idea."

"I don't see this as temporary." Matt meant it. Now that he'd met Gloria, he couldn't imagine going on without her. He wanted to get to know her better. Of course, that included her sons.

"You don't?"

To Matt, Gloria's surprise came over the phone loud and clear.

"Do you?" He asked.

"Everything is just so difficult." He heard her sigh, long and deep. This time she sounded frustrated.

"I know, but I want to know everything about you, Gloria. Part of that is your family." Matt wondered where all this was coming from, but as he kept talking he found that he meant every word, which surprised him; he also felt a surge of happiness, something he hadn't felt with a woman in a long time.

"Part of you is your daughters."

"Right. So it's a good idea. Let's do it in a couple of weekends. My house or yours?" He didn't want her to change her mind.

"Let's do it at mine." Gloria answered. "Then, the boys won't be as inclined to ditch."

"Sounds like a plan."

Matt hoped it would turn out to be a good plan.

****

"I hate not knowing. I wish Liz would tell us definitely whether or not she'll have to let some of us go." Beatrice slathered mayonnaise onto her bread.

Gloria stood at the microwave at work, heating up her frozen dinner of pasta and chicken, one of the healthy ones, though she wondered how healthy it really was since to preserve flavor, salt was used. "I agree."

"You know she hasn't replaced that licensed vocational nurse who quit."

"I think that's just because no one has applied.

60

Besides, I really think we need more registered nurses. They can do more to help with the paperwork, the assessments and orders." Gloria repeated her mantra of hiring more registered nurses than licensed vocational nurses. To her, it made better sense.

"L.V.N.s are cheaper, though." Beatrice munched on her sandwich.

Gloria joined her at the table with her meal. She waited a little for it to cool down, then picked up a forkful of pasta and blew on it before she tasted it.

"What else is going on with you?" Beatrice asked. "Found anyone special yet?"

Feeling her face getting red, Gloria bent down to blow on her food and moved her pasta around with her fork.

"Gloria?" Beatrice persisted. "Are you blushing? Have you met someone? Wow! After all this time. Tell me about him."

"I haven't met anyone." Gloria denied.

"Don't keep me in suspense. Tell me everything." Her friend demanded.

"His name is Matt. He has his own landscaping business. Actually, he's my new gardener."

"Your gardener?" Her friend paused before biting into her sandwich.

"Yes, I met him the Friday I was off, remember? Wayne, my usual gardener, was busy, so he referred Matt to me."

"Wow." Beatrice moved her hand in a *come-on* gesture so Gloria would continue her story.

"We went to eat at Moe's Seafood."

"Yum." Beatrice said.

"Then, Saturday night we went to a masquerade party."

"He's a fast worker, or is it you?"

"Maybe both of us." Gloria cut a piece of chicken and popped it into her mouth.

"Oh, how romantic that ya'll dressed up. What did you go as?"

"He was a gardener and I was 'Mary Mary Quite Contrary'."

"From the nursery rhyme? How did you think of

that? I would never have come up with that? How did you dress?"

"In a blue dress and white apron, plus straw hat and watering can." Gloria smiled. "I guess I thought of the nursery rhyme because of the verse 'how does your garden grow?' Mine wasn't doing too well until Matt came into the picture."

"Is he cute?" Beatrice winked, her thick black eyelash closing over her twinkling eye.

"We sound like high school girls," Gloria giggled.

"Well, is he?"

"Better than cute. He's very attractive and pretty fit for a man who's as old as I am."

"Lucky you. So, have you, you know, cavorted with him?" Beatrice grabbed the chip bag and shook out a few onto a paper plate.

Gloria laughed. "No."

"What are you waiting for? You're not getting any younger."

"These things take time."

"Time, my foot!" Beatrice threw her now empty potato chip bag in the trash. "If you feel it, go for it. Just protect yourself. You never know what disease he might be carrying."

"Oh, Beatrice. What a thought."

"I'm serious. Nowadays, you can't be too careful."

"Well, if he is diseased, I don't want anything to do with him."

Her friend laughed out loud.

"Ladies, excuse me." Carolyn, the receptionist, poked her blonde head into the room. "Liz is here and wants to have another meeting. Are ya'll through with your lunch?"

"Just about." Gloria said, forking in some of her pasta.

"Fifteen minutes, she said. She received a memo from Kedco and wants to read it to us."

Gloria's fear of losing her job settled like a dead weight in her stomach. She threw the rest of her lunch away. Better to find out what was going on than risk throwing up her meal. Besides, she'd lost her appetite. She walked to the conference room.

Liz stood at the head of the conference room table.

The office staff and management sat around. Some of the field staff had been nearby when Carolyn paged them at Liz's request and were present.

"I'm sorry I had to call you in from lunch and from your patients, but this can't wait. I'll post this letter up so the ones who aren't here can read it. It sounds pretty ominous."

As Liz read the letter from Kedco, Gloria tried to make sense of the words—reimbursement for improvement, outcome stats, reduction in staff at the beginning, eventual payoff. Single parents couldn't wait around for eventual payoffs. Not when they had kids in college and about to enter college. What would she do without a job? There was no help for it. Gloria must start looking for another one. And it probably would have to be at another home health agency, even though she'd feel as though she was betraying Liz. But, she had to get a job with the competition. Where else could she get the same amount of pay with her experience? She had been in the business for ten years. Of course, the other home health agencies might be in the same boat. Maybe, no one would be hiring. What a dismal thought.

"I'm not going to start laying people off right away. However, I'll understand if some of you want to start looking for another job. I can't ask you to stay under these circumstances." Liz said and swallowed visibly. Gloria could tell the boss was trying to keep a matter-of-fact attitude. "Thank you for coming. I'll let you know of any new developments."

Silently, Gloria walked to her office.

"Man!" Beatrice said at the door of Gloria's office. "What are we going to do, Gloria?"

"Look for another job?"

"Where? I bet all the other home health agencies are in the same mess."

"That fear did pop into my mind, too, as Liz read the letter."

Beatrice groaned. "I have three kids in school. I can't afford to get less pay. And you know how Chavo's work record goes. Sometimes, he has a job, more times, he doesn't."

"We'll have to play it by ear, I guess. I think I'll begin

to send out resumes, though." Gloria said.

"Maybe I will, too. But where? And you know I put down roots wherever I get a job." Beatrice walked back to her office.

Gloria stared at the pictures of her sons on her desk. Somehow, she'd find a way. She always did. Besides, the worst hadn't happened yet.

Chapter Seven

"Aw, Mom! I don't want a bunch of strangers over here!" Gordy protested. "And girls. Forget 'em."

Ever since Gordy had stopped seeing Kayla he sneered at the subject of girls. Of course, he hadn't told Gloria what had happened. Had he told Dex? No use asking him. Dex wouldn't tell her either and risk losing his brother's trust.

"Matt and I think that it's time the families got together." Gloria stood in the doorway of her son's room. As usual, clothes littered the floor, but today she wasn't interested in that.

"Are you marrying him, Mom?" Dexter asked.

"No, of course not." She hadn't even thought about that. Not really. Had she? "No. We just want to spend some time together with our kids."

"Ya'll spend time together. Why bring us into it?" Gordy asked, not taking his eyes from the video game he was playing.

"Come on, guys! We can make this fun. Matt's girls sound nice."

"Nice and girls don't go together." Gordy said.

"Gordy, don't judge all girls by a bad experience. Not all girls are the same."

"Most girls are."

"It's been my experience, too, Mom." Dex said. "You know the bad experiences I've had. That's why I'm steering clear from them. How old are Matt's daughters?"

"Amber is twelve, Patsy is fifteen and Julia is seventeen just like you, Gordy."

"Yeah, fool, maybe you can connect." Dex teased his brother.

Gordy didn't respond, just frowned at the T.V, then he asked, "Julia?"

"Do you know her?" Gloria looked at her son.

"What's her last name?"

"Cerda." Gloria answered.

"No, I don't think so." Gordy turned back to his game. "The name sounds familiar, but it can't be the same girl."

"Well, anyway, we're doing it. Tomorrow, Saturday. I'm buying the food. I don't want to be cooking. We'll get barbecue from Rudy's."

"Yeah." Dex said. "That's the best, unless I do it myself."

Gloria laughed, happy that at least Dex wasn't upset with her. Neither was Gordy, but he was hurt. That girl had hurt her baby. And she wondered how. She walked to the kitchen to refill her glass with water. She'd just have to wait until he was ready to tell her.

****

"This is Julia." Matt said and pointed to a beautiful girl with luscious long black hair. "And that's Patsy."

Gloria smiled at the slightly pudgy girl with black hair as she stood at the entrance of her home.

"And the little one is Amber."

"I'm not little."

"Hi, Amber." Gloria smiled at the thin girl. For a second, Gloria was taken back to when she was twelve—shy and in glasses since second grade. She was smart, too, and everyone called her *the brain* when she just wanted to be popular both with the girls and the boys.

"Well," Gloria shook her memories away. "These are my sons, Dex and Gordy."

"Gordy?" Julia asked. "What kind of name is that?"

Matt shook her sons' hands. "Forgive my daughter. She's shy around new people."

"His name is Gordon Daniel." Gloria said.

Dex smiled, but Gordy frowned and left the living room.

"We're off to a rousing start," Gloria commented as Matt's daughters and Dex went outside.

"I told them about your roses. They're going to check my work," Matt smiled.

Gloria looked around for Gordy.

"Relax. Once we sit down to eat, things will get smoother." Matt sauntered outside as well.

In a few minutes, Patsy returned. "The roses look nice. My Dad said you almost killed them. Don't you know

66

about plants?"

"Not much. But I'm learning." Gloria said as she spooned potato salad on paper plates.

"Can I help you?" Patsy volunteered.

Gloria looked around the kitchen at the containers of beans, potato salad and creamed corn with the familiar logo of a barbecue pit on the label Rudy's Barbecue was known for, then at the table. "You can fill those paper cups with ice. What do you like to drink? I've got soda, juice and water."

"Bottled water?"

"Yes."

"Good. That's all Julia drinks. Me, I like soda. What kind do you have?"

Gloria finished with the potato salad and started serving beans. "Sprite, Coke, orange, root beer."

"Root beer? Yuk!"

"When I was growing up, root beer was a treat for us." Gloria said. "But, actually, I don't like it anymore, my sons do."

"I'll have orange."

Matt entered the room followed by his daughters.

"Where's Dex?" Gloria looked through the dining room window.

"He's talking to the neighbor."

"I'll go get Gordy." Gloria finished serving the potato salad and went to her son's room.

"I don't want to go out there, Mom, and you can't make me."

"Come on, Gordy. You have to eat."

"I'll wait until she leaves."

"Please, Gordy. Don't be difficult."

Gordy stared at her. He knew how much this party meant to her. She had told him. So as she waited, he stood up from the bed and followed her to the table.

"This looks better than my lasagna, right, girls?" Matt asked.

"You cooked lasagna?" Gloria wondered, impressed.

"Yeah. My most delicious meal yet, right, girls?"

"Right, Dad." Julia said and stared at Gordy, who only looked down at his plate.

Matt tore into some brisket. "Very good."

"Yes, it is. The sauce is a bit spicy, but it wouldn't be the same barbecue without it," Gloria commented.

She looked around the table, her boys mixed in with Matt's girls. Would they ever be comfortable with each other? Right now, it didn't look like it. Gordy wouldn't even look at Julia.

"We watched some movies last weekend." Matt said. "Tell Gloria about them. I'm sure she'd like to hear about them. Romantic comedies."

"Oh yeah? My favorite. Which ones did you watch?" Gloria began eating.

Patsy answered. It seemed she had really enjoyed all of them. T.V. and movie fanatic, like she was, Gloria remembered. Amber interjected her opinion once in awhile. Julia didn't participate in the conversation. Dex commented about one of the movies since it featured one of his favorite actors.

"I felt sorry for that girl, the one who couldn't fit in," Amber commented.

"That was you all the way, Amber," Julia said.

"And that mean popular girl was you," Amber yelled and shoved Julia.

"Girls." Matt gave his daughters a warning look.

"It's amazing how things never change." Gloria stood to clear off some of the empty paper plates. "When I was a girl, I was just like you, Amber. I joined the band just so I could be part of a group."

"Geeks." Dex smiled, teasing her as he always did about her band days.

"And proud of it, too." She grinned at her son.

Gloria noticed that Amber stared at her with a hopeful look on her face, but then Julia elbowed her and she turned to her sister and pulled her hair.

"Gordy, I know you're a senior in high school. What about you, Dex?" Matt asked.

Dex forked a helping of beans into his mouth. Once he was finished, he finally answered, "I'm in college, last year."

"Good for you." Matt continued eating.

Gloria looked down at her plate, beans, potato salad, brisket. *Please Dex, say something else.*

"I'm majoring in Graphic Design." Dex volunteered.

Gloria inwardly sighed with relief.

"Sometimes, I wish I'd gone to college."

"I'm not going," Julia said. "I want to travel."

Gordy shook his head.

"What?" The girl demanded.

"I didn't say anything," Gordy said.

"Not with your voice, but your attitude said a lot. What's wrong with traveling?"

"An education is important," Matt offered.

Gloria saw her sons grin. Poor Matt. She hoped he wouldn't start preaching about education. Her boys would have a field day about it later. Thankfully, Matt stopped there. The conversation centered on Julia's travel plans.

Once the meal was over, Gloria cleaned up. She told the girls to go outside to the patio table and she'd take out bowls of ice cream. She needed a reprieve—to be by herself for a few minutes. Did she really need this stress in her life? Looking out the patio door, she saw Matt fiddling around with one of her rose bushes. Her heart skipped a beat. Yes, it was worth it.

Dex and Gordy were outside, too, but not at the patio table. They were by the shed where the treadmill and exercise bicycle were. She continued spooning ice cream into bowls.

"Gloria?" Amber slid the patio door open and came in.

"Hi, Amber. Want to help me?"

"Can I ask you about something?" Amber pushed around one of the bowls of ice cream.

"Sure, sweetie." Gloria said with a smile.

"You were a girl once, right?"

Gloria nodded. "I believe so, yes."

"I'm sorry. I didn't mean to insult you." Amber stared at Gloria with a contrite look.

"Don't worry about it. What's on your mind?"

"I've asked a lot of people about this and no one seems to be able to help me."

Was this what she hadn't been able to tell Matt? Gloria felt honored that Amber sought her advice.

"Go ahead, Amber, I'm listening." Gloria looked at the girl.

"I'm afraid."

"So many things to be afraid of at twelve. Tell me

your fear." Gloria continued to fill bowls with ice cream.

"You promise you won't laugh at me?"

"I promise."

"My mom promised, too, and she laughed. Please don't laugh at me." Amber put her hands together.

"I won't laugh, sweetie. Tell me. What are you afraid of?"

"I'm afraid of...of..." Amber stammered and sat on a nearby chair.

Gloria waited. Poor girl! It must be horrible, whatever it was.

"I'm afraid of stinking when I'm on my period. And that everyone will know I'm on it. And that I'm going to bleed all over myself. Oh, I wish I weren't a girl." Amber spoke in a rush, then hung her head and wouldn't look at Gloria.

Gloria looked down at the little girl's black hair in the ponytail and put down the ice cream scoop and pulled her up from the chair and hugged her.

"Oh darling, I felt exactly the same way when I was your age."

"You did?" Amber's voice sounded muffled since her mouth was against Gloria's chest.

"Yes. But it'll get better, I promise. Just stay as clean as you can. Bathe every day. Change your pads, or tampons, whatever you use, regularly. And—you can also spray a whole bottle of perfume, or body spray on yourself every time you go anywhere."

"Really?"

"That's what I used to do." Gloria said and pushed back stray hairs from around Amber's face.

Amber looked at her with wonder in her eyes.

"Spray a lot on your chest, then every time you look down you'll smell the perfume and you'll feel more confident. And, of course, never wear white when you're on your period. Wear dark colors. You know, another thing I used to do is I would wear jackets. That way if an accident did occur, I could always tie it around my waist to hide it."

"Come to my room. I want to give you something." Gloria led the girl down the hallway.

"I like your room. All by yourself. I have to share a

room with Patsy and she hogs all the space." Amber looked around Gloria's room with a grin on her childish face.

Gloria smiled, thankful that she had straightened up in there. The sky blue comforter and matching window treatments, chosen for the calming color, did make the room look nice. She led Amber to the dresser at the end of her bed. She sat down and patted the space next to her. When Amber joined her, she pulled out the top drawer. Pulling out three small bottles of perfume, she told Amber, "Pick out the one you like."

"Really?" Amber put her hands up to her mouth and jumped a little on the bed.

"Really."

The little girl tried each scent, spraying it on each wrist. "I like this one." She looked at Gloria with hope on her face.

"You can have it."

"Thank you, Gloria." Amber threw her arms around Gloria.

"You're welcome, sweetie."

"What's this?" Julia said and frowned at the doorway of Gloria's room. "What are you doing, Amber? She's not our mom."

"Of course, I'm not, Julia. I would never try to take your mom's place."

"Amber's weird. Whatever she said to you, forget it." Julia frowned at her sister.

Amber looked at Gloria with a stricken expression.

"No, I won't forget it, but it's up to Amber to tell you what we talked about if she wants to."

Amber smiled with a grateful expression on her face and went outside. Julia followed her without a smile or a word to Gloria.

Gloria returned to the kitchen, finished with the ice cream and placed the bowls on a tray. At the refrigerator, she took out chocolate syrup and strawberry topping and placed those on the tray as well. As she slid the patio door open, she heard raised voices.

Gordy said, "You're just like all the other girls. Aren't you dating Andy? He's a friend of mine. I wonder what he would think if I told him what you just did."

"I'm just trying to be friendly."

"Yeah, right." Gordy left by the side gate door.

"Gordy?" Gloria called her son.

"I'm leaving, Mom. I can't stand this."

"Gordy?"

"Let him go, Gloria." Matt said.

In the next few minutes, she heard the sound of Gordy's speakers as he turned on his car and left.

Gloria served the ice cream, no one at the table talked. "Anybody want toppings? Chocolate or strawberry?"

Amber took the chocolate syrup and drizzled it over her ice cream. "Thank you."

Gloria wanted to break the silence, but couldn't think of a thing to say. Matt frowned the whole time. Dex excused himself and took his ice cream inside.

After the ice cream was finished, Gloria picked up the bowls and tray to take them back inside.

"We'd better go," Matt said when she returned.

Gloria noticed that Julia was restless, tapping her fingernails on the table, Patsy sighed.

As they walked inside and to the front door, Gloria said, "I'm glad you came, girls. Please come again."

Patsy smiled at her, but Julia ignored her and walked out the door.

"Thank you, Gloria. I'll remember everything you said," Amber said, as she and Patsy walked out.

"What was that about?" Matt looked out the door at his daughters.

"Amber and I talked. I think she told me what she tried to tell you the other night."

"Really?" Matt said and his shoulders stiffened. "My daughter told you what she couldn't tell me?"

"Yes. It was a girl thing. I couldn't have told my dad either." Gloria tried to soften the blow.

"So, my daughter talked to you?" Matt's body radiated tension.

"Matt, are you angry?"

"No. At least she got it off her chest and she seems happier about it." Matt wouldn't look at her.

"You are mad." Gloria furrowed her brow and almost wished she hadn't interfered, but Amber had sought her out.

"No, dammit! I'm not mad. Just disappointed that she couldn't talk to me about it."

"Your little girl is growing up."

"I suppose." Matt's stern stance didn't change.

"What happened between Julia and Gordy? I didn't hear how the argument started."

"Your son called my daughter a bad name," Matt said, hitting a fist into his open palm.

"Oh dear. I'll tell him to apologize to her."

"Very eventful day we've had."

"Very. Should we do it again?" Gloria asked, even though she wondered if it was a good idea.

"Maybe not for a while." Apparently, Matt felt the same way.

"Okay." Did Matt mean for them to stop seeing each other?

Chapter Eight

"Gordy, what happened with Julia?" Gloria sat on her son's bed.

"I don't want to talk about it."

"It's not even about Julia is it? It's about Kayla, right?"

"Who's that? I don't even remember her."

"*Mijo*, you need to talk about it."

Gordy rolled over on his bed and covered his eyes with his fists.

"Sweetie?" Gloria saw the trickle of tears at the corners of his eyes. When he moved his hands, she saw that his eyes were red.

"Don't tell the wuss. Then, he'll say I am the wuss."

Gloria felt as if her heart had shattered, just looking at how hurt her baby was due to some girl being mean to him. How dare she? Who did she think she was anyway?

"I liked her, Mom. I thought she liked me, too."

"She probably did, Gordy. Girls can be fickle, though. Both your Aunt Lynda and I were. And we never thought about how the poor guy felt. I remember one boy. He liked me more than I liked him and I was always playing with him. Breaking dates and not letting him kiss me."

"Aw, Mom! I don't want to hear about that."

"Sorry." Gloria laughed and tousled her son's hair, which was soft since he hadn't put any gel in it yet. He tended to slather it on.

"What exactly happened with Kayla?"

"She dumped me. I feel so bad." Gordy covered his face again.

"Tell me, son."

"There I was, full of plans for us to date during our senior year, go to the prom. I was even planning what to get her for Valentine's Day. She said she didn't want to be tied down her last year in school. I hate to think of what I did next."

"What?" Gloria's heart contracted at the possibilities.

"I begged her to stay with me. Begged, Mom. I'm such a loser." Gordy turned his head into the pillow.

"You're not a loser. You were thinking with your heart."

"Now, I have to see her all through the school term." Gordy's words sounded muffled with the pillow covering his mouth. "Kayla betrayed me. I found out that she's dated practically every senior she's met this summer. I guess she really wants to enjoy her senior year."

"Was that the reason you were mean to Julia?"

"Part of it." Gordy turned to face her.

"Go on."

"She said she was just being friendly, but I know better."

"She made a pass at you?"

"What's that? Oh, make the moves on me? No, she and her sister, Patsy, just started talking about all the guys she dates. I thought she was going out with Andy. You know Andy. He's been here a couple of times. The other day he told me about this girl he met. Julia. He's really into her." Gordy rubbed his eyes.

"Don't do that, Gordy. Your eyes will get even redder," Gloria admonished her son. "Yes, I remember you said the name sounded familiar."

"Yeah. You can see why I called her, well...what I called her."

"You're going to have to apologize to her, you know?"

"No, I'm not. I'm not sorry. I said it because it's the truth."

"She was a guest in our house, *mijo*, and we don't mistreat people in our home."

"She has to apologize to me, too." Gordy looked at the T.V.

"Why?"

"For being a girl."

"Gordy, you're being silly."

"Can't help it. Girls make me so angry. This Matt guy has three of them. How can he stand it?"

"He probably had the same experience you did when he was a boy and he was blessed with three girls that he can mold into great women." Gloria smiled at her son.

"He's not doing his job."

"I'm going to see how I can set up another get-together so you can apologize to Julia." Gloria stood up.

"Aw!"

"And I'm sorry about Kayla, sweetie. You'll meet another girl someday and she'll make you forget Kayla and you'll realize girls can be special."

"Don't hold your breath." Gordy said, not giving an inch.

****

"Hey!" Matt's voice sounded over the answering machine.

Gloria picked up the cordless phone from its cradle on the small wood table by the kitchen. "Hi, Matt." She swallowed.

"I'm training a new guy today. Remember that one I told you about who never showed? Well, I had to replace him," Matt paused.

Gloria didn't respond, she just stared outside toward her garden with unseeing eyes. Her roses weren't brown and black anymore. She had Matt to thank for that. And for so much more. Relationships were so hard, though.

"Yeah, I'm training him today. So, how are you?"

"Fine." Gloria wanted to respond to Matt. His voice on the phone was making her body tingle in places she'd forgotten could tingle. But, he owed her an apology.

"I'm sorry."

"Oh?"

"Last night at the barbecue, I was jealous that Amber talked to you."

"Oh, really?" Gloria sat down on a dining room chair.

"Give me another chance, rose princess. Or, should I call you *Mary, Mary Quite Contrary*?"

Gloria bit back a laugh. His daughter needed another woman to listen to her. A man wouldn't understand. He should know that. But then, why should he? He was a father, not a man where Amber was concerned. His daughter had a problem and he couldn't help her.

"Gloria? Are you going to accept my apology?"

She relented. He sounded so forlorn. "I shouldn't make it so easy for you. I was only trying to help. I didn't approach Amber. She came to me."

"I know she did. She scolded me for acting like a bear with you, as she put it. She was the one who suggested rather strongly that I apologize."

"So, this apology wasn't your idea?"

"Let's just say the thoughts came at the same time. So?"

"Okay. I accept your apology. I talked to Gordy about Julia. He owes her an apology."

"Maybe we shouldn't have barbecues anymore. Too much apologizing required afterwards."

"Right? Why don't we go to the coast, just you and me, and you can barbecue fish."

"You don't like fish."

"Ummm...but I like you."

"I like you, too."

His words sent a flutter to Gloria's stomach.

"I'd like to seal this apology with a kiss, but— *chingado*! Here comes Jaime. He's my trainee. He's ready for the next test."

"Are you actually testing these poor guys?"

"Of course. You never know when they'll have to help a lady with dead roses."

"Yeah. Yeah."

"I'd like to see my lady with the dead roses tonight. How about it?"

"Well, my roses aren't dead anymore. And I'm going to a church festival tonight."

"What? You'd rather go there than be with me?"

"Why don't you join me. I donated a bunch of my roses for decorations and prizes. After all, it is St. Rose Church and the festival is the Roses' Fiesta."

"I've created a monster."

"Thank you so much for my roses."

"I'll see you tonight."

****

Gloria parked in the church parking lot. She hoped Gordy and Dex would show up. She left them watching wrestling on TV, but they promised after it was over, they would come. The sound of Tejano music, a polka, filled the air when she got out of the car. Maybe, she and Matt could dance, though he told her he didn't know how to dance. He could learn from her. Smells of fajitas, beef skirt steak seasoned and grilled, and gorditas frying assailed her nostrils. Gordy loved those, corn meal pockets filled with chicken, beans and cheese or beef. Her son preferred the chicken with lots of cheese. As she walked nearer, she saw the Roses' Fiesta Committee had been able to get the small Ferris wheel for the kids. The ride was always a good money maker.

"Gloria! Over here!" Lynda, her sister, called out. When they were growing up, people had commented on their likeness, but now even after four kids, Lynda's slim figure didn't show it. Her husband, John, a slender man who wore wire-framed glasses, stood beside her.

"Hi. Glad ya'll came. I'm not sure the boys are coming and I was afraid I'd be wandering around here all alone."

"What about Matt?" Lynda asked, brushing her light brown hair back from her face.

"He said he'd be here, but I'm not sure when. It's already dark, so he should be finished with his job." Gloria looked around the festival and saw the colorful booths and crowds of people, both adults and children.

"He works on Sundays?" John's dark eyebrows rose above his glasses.

"Lately. He's shorthanded."

"Let's go get something to eat," John suggested. "I've got tickets."

"Oh, that's right." Gloria turned to the ticket booth at the entrance to the festival grounds. "We need tickets. I'll be right back."

"Don't worry about it." Her brother-in-law said. "My treat."

"I want to dance, too. Can we dance?" Lynda asked her husband, as Gloria followed them to the food booths.

"Maybe. Later."

"You always make me wait," Lynda complained.

Gloria smiled. Her sister and John had been married for years and had a special relationship even with four kids.

"Where are the kids?"

"Lisa and Abel had plans with their friends. Yolanda is home working on a school project that she left until the last minute. J.L is here somewhere, probably playing the basketball game," Lynda told her.

Gloria looked over toward the basketball game at the entrance of the grounds and sure enough she saw her nephew, John Lewis, nicknamed J.L. ever since he was a baby. "Well, let's go eat. I can't wait for a fajita taco."

"Gloria! Dear! We need you." Minnie O'Brien, the committee chairman, walked at a fast pace toward her, the roses on her hat fluttered in the slight breeze in the hot and humid air.

"Hi, Minnie. What's up?" Gloria asked, hoping there was nothing wrong with the roses she had donated.

"The lady who signed up to man the roses booth didn't show. I'd do it myself, but I already have to go help out at the bottle toss. Someone else didn't show up over there. It makes me so mad when people volunteer and then don't come."

Gloria forbore to tell Minnie that it was probably because she practically forced people to volunteer. Some only did so to get away from her. "I'll be right there. Let me just get one fajita taco. You know those run out pretty fast."

"Thank you, dear. I knew I could count on you. Hello, Lynda, John. Must go now." Minnie left in a rush, almost losing her hat on a low tree branch as she passed.

John laughed. "Did you see that? Now, that would have been a good picture if she had lost it."

"Oh you!" Lynda tapped him on the upper arm. "Don't be so mean. She's a good person. Don't make fun of her."

"I know, but it's still funny." John's eyes gleamed with mirth.

When she finally got through the line and got her taco, Gloria took one bite after spooning on a little bit of guacamole, avocado mixed with tomato, onion and spices and put on just a little bit of pico de gallo.

"Watch out for that *pico*, the *jalapenos* are really hot," Lynda warned. "That's why I got more tomatoes."

"Oh, you're right." Gloria said as the spiciness of the pepper bit her tongue. "I need a soda." She waved to Lynda and John. "Come over to the roses booth when you get a chance. I'd better get over there."

Only stopping to get a soda at the drinks booth, Gloria walked toward the roses booth, situated in the center of the festival grounds. Minnie was there, but left as soon as she saw Gloria.

Single roses in green tissue paper and rose corsages with baby's breaths also covered the board behind her. Each rose had a number corresponding to the number squares on the counter. The aim of the game was to buy number squares and at the turn of the roulette wheel, the winning number would win the prize. Her roses looked beautiful. Gloria finished her taco and put her face in one particular arrangement of red roses. The soft scent perfumed the air around her. Matt had one of the greenest thumbs she knew. Her roses were healthy and were prizes at a church festival. She grinned and hugged the vase, which held a rose.

"Hey, I'm jealous of that rose." Matt walked up to the booth.

"Matt, you came."

"I told you I'd see you tonight."

"I thought you meant later on tonight, after the festival."

"Couldn't stay away from you for that long."

"How much does this game cost?" A teenage boy with a girl leaning far too close to him asked.

"Four tickets."

"Tickets?"

"Yes, go over to that booth at the entrance to the festival. Each ticket is twenty-five cents."

"We'll be back."

"They did have good timing, didn't they?" Matt grinned.

"Come inside the booth," Gloria invited.

Matt entered the booth and grabbed Gloria around the waist. She leaned close, but then squirmed away when a group of customers walked up.

Two girls walked away with two single roses each. Gloria watched them leave with pride in her eyes.

Matt hugged her again.

"Thank you so much. This is one of the happiest times of my life. My roses are prizes."

"I always like to make the ladies happy."

"All the ladies?" Gloria turned into his arms.

"Just one particular lady." Matt kissed her and his

warm lips on hers swept her away from the noisy crowd at the festival and the music of the chicken dance.

"I didn't think churches allowed kissing booths."

Gloria heard him through the fog of losing her senses in Matt's kiss. What was she doing? In a public place, too? And her son had arrived. Gloria pushed Matt away.

"Gordy. Do you want to play the game and win one of my roses?"

"Naw! I'm going to go get a hamburger." Gordy would have left if Gloria hadn't stopped him.

"Gordy, don't be rude. Say hello to Matt."

"Hello." He said it quickly, without looking at Matt and proceeded to leave.

"Do you want to try your luck at the roses booths? Your mom's roses are pretty nice. And I get the credit." Matt suggested.

Gordy frowned, "My mom had been growing her roses long before you came into the picture."

Gloria admonished her son, but he walked away.

"Did Dex come with you?" Gloria yelled after him.

"Yeah, he's over there with J.L. at the basketball game." Her son answered without looking back.

"I'm sorry about that. I'll talk to him about his manners. He's usually not like that."

"Forget about it. It's hard for all of us right now. We'll get through it." Matt shrugged.

"I hope so."

"Hey, I want to win a rose for my sweetheart here." John walked up to the booth with Lynda.

"Sure thing." Gloria introduced Matt to her sister and her husband.

John tried five times before he won a rose corsage for Lynda. With a grin, he pinned it on her blouse. "Beautiful." John kissed Lynda.

Gloria smiled, happy for her sister. She glanced at Matt and he smiled at her.

"Do you have to stay here all night?" Matt asked when John and Lynda had left and no one was at the booth.

"I hope not. I want to dance a cumbia with you."

"I can't dance that, remember?" Matt reminded her.

"I'll teach you."

"I think I can manage a polka."

"Maybe they'll play country-western and you can teach me how to two-step. I've never learned that."

"You live in Texas and don't know how to two-step?" Matt exclaimed in mock horror.

"I'm here, Gloria. What happened to Sandra?" Hannah, one of the members of the Ladies' Society walked up to the booth. "Oh, that's a long walk from the parking lot." The stout lady paused to catch her breath.

Gloria assumed Sandra must be the one who should have been at the booth. "She didn't show. Minnie asked me to step in."

"Thank you for that. Oh, these roses are beautiful." Hannah held a corsage up to her nose. "They smell good, too."

"My roses." Gloria smiled. "I had a very good gardener this year."

"Send him my way. My roses are dying for some reason."

"This is him. Matt, Hannah."

"Oh. Did you come to see how the roses were doing?" Hannah asked. "Why that's wonderful."

Gloria laughed. "Matt is not only my gardener. He's my...friend."

"Oh, friend, okay," Hannah smiled. "Well, go off with you. I'll take over. Go have some fun. Dance."

"Do you want to dance?" Matt asked as they walked away.

"Yes."

Climbing up to the cement dance floor nearby, Matt led her up the stairs and took her in his arms for the polka. "I'm not sure I can do this."

"Just twirl me around." Gloria said and moved her feet to the music. "It's kinda like a fast waltz."

"I don't know how to waltz," Matt admitted, but got into the spirit of the dance and even tried a cumbia. Gloria swayed to the rhythm of the beat and this time twirled on her own around Matt.

After several minutes of dancing, Gloria suggested they sit down. Her heart seemed to be beating very fast. She touched her cheeks and they felt hot. Was she flushed?

"Are you okay, Gloria?" Matt asked.

"I'm fine. Maybe, some water." Gloria took deep breaths to calm her heart rate and catch her breath. Oh God! What was the matter with her?

She got up to follow Matt to the drinks booth and tripped over a tree root. Gloria stood up and touched her knee. She knew she had scraped it, could feel the burning sensation of broken skin. Dizziness overwhelmed her. She had to sit down. She looked around and her ears were ringing. Was she having a stroke? Oh no!

"Gloria?" Lynda asked, holding her hand. "What's the matter?" Her sister led her to a table.

"I just have to sit down for a minute. I tripped and fell." When she sat down, Gloria put her head between her legs to get rid of the dizziness.

"Again? You need to watch where you're going, sis? Do you think your blood pressure is up? Did you take your medicine today?"

"Medicine?" Matt handed Gloria the water. "Are you sick?"

Lynda began to explain, but Gloria interrupted, "I'm not sick. I just got overheated. It's too hot to be dancing." Gloria drank some water and frowned at Lynda and warned her with her expression not to say anything more.

Chapter Nine

No one was at Home Nursing yet when Gloria arrived. She went to her office to put her purse down and grabbed her glass. Turning on the water in the small kitchen, she filled her glass to make iced tea. She heard the door open and close.

Beatrice walked in with a rustle of plastic bags. "I brought my lunch today. This week I'm going to be good. I'm spending too much on lunch. Chavo lost his job again."

"Oh no."

"We had it out Friday night when I got home from work to find him sitting on the couch. He had been there all day and didn't bother to call me to tell me he'd been laid off. I'm so mad I could spit. That was my weekend. How was yours?"

Gloria finished making her glass of tea. "I almost fainted at the church festival."

"What happened? Did your boyfriend kiss your breath away?" Her friend grinned before she took a sip of coffee.

"I wish." Gloria huffed. "I tripped, fell and made a complete fool of myself in front of everybody there, including Matt."

"I'm sorry. Are you hurt?"

"Well, I did skin my knee, but my pride hurt the most." She took a sip of tea. "Wonder if Annie will bring those scones I like today? She hasn't done so in awhile."

Beatrice said, "I love the muffins."

"I'll have to make do with these fruit-bars. One apple and one strawberry."

"Should you eat both?"

"I am today."

"Uh oh. What's up? Something besides the fall? You know, it's not always candy and roses with men in the picture."

"Good morning, ladies." Annie Myers hurried in,

laden down with folders and her nurses' bag. She also had a box of goodies from the bakery by her house.

"Oh, Annie, you didn't?" Gloria exclaimed and opened the box. She saw the lemon and cranberry scones in there along with muffins and pastries, but she had eyes only for the scones.

"Yum! I have to eat at least half of one. Don't tell anyone. I'll eat salads for lunch and dinner." Gloria bit into the doughy lemony scone.

"I like the banana nut muffins." Beatrice stated. "I don't know how you can eat those things. They're too bready."

"You don't know what's good." She bit into her scone again. "By the way, I like your haircut." Annie usually had her ash blond hair pinned up in a haphazard way, as being the nurse supervisor was time-consuming and stressful. Today, though, her hair was short and styled to curl under.

"You like? I thought it was time for a change. How's your blood pressure, Gloria?" Annie asked.

"It's been normal lately. I feel a little better now that the doctor adjusted my meds."

"She fell last night." Beatrice walked out of the kitchen with her muffin. "Tell me more later."

"You fell?" Annie asked, her blue eyes wide in concern.

"It was nothing, just skinned my knee, but I did feel dizzy."

"Let me check your blood pressure." Annie opened her nurses' bag and got out her stethoscope and blood pressure cuff.

"Well, it's 110 over 80. That's good." Annie pulled at the cuff and unstuck the Velcro and took it from Gloria's arm. "When are you seeing your doctor?"

"I'm going on Friday for an EKG, then I'll see him."

"An EKG?" Annie looked concerned again.

"Just as a precaution. He just wants to make sure everything is fine since I haven't been feeling my best, but I think it's just the meds."

"It doesn't hurt to be sure." Annie left the kitchen.

Gloria followed Annie down the hallway. "No, it doesn't."

When Gloria reached her office, Beatrice called her name. "So, anything else happen this weekend?"

She was tempted to tell her friend about her refusal to tell Matt about her health issues, but she decided not to. Instead she told her about her job search. "No, not really. Listen, I'm going to send out resumes today."

"You are?" Beatrice hurriedly swallowed her coffee.

"Yes, I can't wait around to see what happens. I need to do something. So, I'm sending out resumes."

"To other home health agencies?"

"Also to bookstores and libraries. See what happens. Lynda always tells me everything happens for a reason. Maybe this is my chance to find a job I really want."

"You're not happy here?" Beatrice wrinkled her nose.

"I am, for the most part. But, I've been here for ten years. I'm ready for a change." Gloria turned around to go to her office. "Besides, I don't want to wait until it's too late."

"We are getting older," Beatrice agreed.

"Older and sicker? Who knows what can happen to us?" Gloria said. "Better to do what you really want to do and not think about it too much."

As Gloria turned on her computer, she wondered if she should follow that advice regarding Matt, too. What if she had the ingredients for a great sexual encounter and she waited around too long to make a decision? She didn't want to just have sex. She'd had that experience a few years back. She knew she couldn't do that again. With Matt, she knew it wasn't just about sex, though as she thought of his body, she sighed. She remembered how she had felt in the truck with him—before she stopped him.

Carolyn's voice on the intercom interrupted her. "Gloria, line two."

Gloria picked up her phone.

"Hi." Matt's voice.

Had she conjured him up with her thoughts? "Hi."

"I'm calling to invite you to a birthday party?"

"Your birthday?"

"No, that's passed. Amber's thirteenth. I can't believe it. My baby girl is a teenager."

"Oh, how sweet. Is she having a big party with her friends?" Gloria logged into her computer.

"No, just the family. Thankfully, not my sisters and brothers, though. We'll do that another time."

Gloria breathed a quiet sigh of relief.

Matt continued, "I asked Angela to let the girls come over Friday night so we could celebrate Amber's birthday together. The actual date is today, but she's happy to celebrate all week if we want. She gave me her birthday list."

Gloria laughed as she listened to Matt. "Just like my boys. Gordy starts planning his birthday party right after Easter and it's in June."

"So, can you come? Bring your sons, too."

"I don't know about those boys, especially Gordy."

"He still needs to apologize, right?"

"Yes, he does need to do that." Gloria's body stiffened at that. As if she needed reminding that her son had insulted his daughter. She picked up a folder and threw it with unnecessary force into her stack-up tray.

"I'm sorry. You're angry with me, aren't you?"

"No, you're absolutely right. Gordy does need to apologize." Gloria sat back in her chair and took a couple of deep breaths.

"I can hear a bit of hissing in your voice."

"I'm just breathing deeply. I'm fine."

"Okay. See you Friday night."

Gloria held the phone to her ear for a couple of seconds, then hung it up. Things were difficult. Was all of this stress worth it? Did she have the energy for this?

****

"Boys, I'm home." Gloria closed the front door with her foot. Her hands were holding countless plastic bags from the grocery store. "Come help me. I think I over-did it with buying food again."

Gordy came jogging up to grab some bags and took them to the dining table. Dex followed his brother. "Any more stuff in the car?"

"Yes, a few more bags. Oh, and the cases of bottled water."

Both her sons went outside. Gloria busied herself in putting up the groceries. Tonight, she decided they'd have sandwiches. Quick and easy. After the busyness of the grocery store, she didn't feel like cooking.

When her sons returned, she said, "I thought we'd have sandwiches. What do you think?"

"Did you buy that special bread?" Gordy asked.

"You mean those submarine rolls? Yes, I did. I got turkey for you and roast beef for you, Dex. Is that okay?"

"Yeah. I hope we have mustard."

"Oh, mustard. I forgot you told me to get some."

"There's enough in here, I think." Dex took out a small jar from the refrigerator.

"It hasn't expired, has it?" Gloria adjusted her glasses to examine the jar.

"Mustard doesn't expire, does it?" Dex asked.

"Well, maybe a 'sell by' date. Yeah, it should be okay, the 'sell by' date is a couple months away. Smell it first before you put it on the bread."

While Gloria made her turkey sandwich, her sons made theirs at the dining table. For awhile, all she heard were the sounds of the knife against the mustard jar, the pop of the container as Gordy opened the turkey and the pouring of juice into glasses.

"Let's eat," Gloria said. "Oh, the chips."

When she sat down at the table again, Gloria bit into her sandwich, then asked, "How was your day?"

"Okay." Gordy answered and busied himself eating.

"I went to the bookstore and got my books. I was able to get a few school supplies with the leftover money, spirals, pens, things like that. Those books are expensive and sometimes we don't even use them in class," Dex said.

"When do classes start?" Gloria took some chips from the bag, supposedly baked, but less fat meant more salt, so she just got a few.

"In three weeks," Dex gulped down some juice.

"I start in two weeks. My free time is coming to an end." Gordy said.

"It's your last year, son. Make it a good one."

"I just want school to be over."

"I loved school. I never wanted it to end." Gloria sipped her juice.

"Yes, we know, Mom," Dex grinned, then he sobered up. "Hey, Mom, a doctor's office called you about an appointment. Are you sick?"

About to bite into her sandwich, she stopped. Should

she tell her sons about her blood pressure? Lynda advised her not to. Somehow, she felt her sons had a right to know. What if she keeled over? They wouldn't know what had happened.

"Mom, what's up with that?" Dex looked at her with a look of concern.

"I meant to tell you, boys, but I didn't want to worry you. And it's really nothing. I just have to take medication, watch what I eat and exercise."

"I noticed you were out at the shed more." Gordy picked up his sandwich.

"Are you sick?" Dex repeated.

"I've got high blood pressure. I just need to go to the doctor every four to six weeks for follow-ups. I'm going for an EKG on Friday." At her son's questioning looks, she explained, "It's a way to measure how my heart is pumping."

"Is it surgery? Are you going to be put to sleep?" Dex sat up straighter in his chair.

"Oh no, I'm not." She quickly corrected her son's thinking. "It'll be done at an imaging center and they'll just hook me up to a machine with wires and it'll spit out a printout, which the doctor will interpret and let me know whether my heart is normal or not. And it will be. Please don't worry about it, okay? It's just a precaution. I feel fine."

Her sons looked at her with concern in their faces, but then they visibly relaxed. "If you say so, Mom." Dex said.

"I say so. Hey, I've got something to tell you. Or, rather ask you," Gloria began.

The boys continued eating. "Before you do, Mom, Dad called today." Dex said.

"Your dad? You haven't heard from him in awhile, have you?" Gloria asked, trying not to sound critical. Eddie didn't deserve his sons' love with the little attention he paid them. However, she knew her sons, especially Dex, liked to hear from their dad.

"I told him about Matt," Dex confessed.

Gloria's heart flip-flopped. Not that she wanted to hide the fact that she was dating from Eddie. Still, he had been her husband. "Why did you do that?"

"He called the night you went to the festival, before Gordo and I went. And I just told him."

Gloria wondered if Dex still harbored a wish that she and Eddie would get back together. She supposed he would always hope. Her heart hurt at the thought of her son's desire, but she couldn't live with Eddie. She'd tried for several years. Marriage, commitment of any kind, wasn't Eddie's cup of tea. Honesty wasn't either. The thought made her cringe. She hadn't been totally honest with Matt and that bothered her. But what was it with him and illness? Besides, high blood pressure was manageable.

"Are you angry, Mom?" Dex looked at her with a worried expression on his face.

She smiled. "No, *mijo*. The fact that I'm seeing Matt isn't a secret. I guess I feel a bit strange because he was my husband—and he is your dad. Seems weird."

"Tell me about it." Dex said and Gordy nodded.

Anyway, I wanted to tell you about an invitation we received. Matt called to invite us to his daughter's birthday party."

"Aw!" Gordy groaned and put his sandwich down.

"Which daughter?" Dex asked. "Gordo's favorite one?"

"No, not Julia's, though you still have to apologize to her. It's Amber's thirteenth birthday party."

"I don't want to go to some girl's party," Gordy said.

"I'm too old for that stuff, Mom," Dex said. "I think I have plans with Tony."

"Guys, come on. Do this for me. It's important."

"Mom, what's going on with this Matt character?" Dex asked and looked at Gordy.

Gloria's stomach fluttered. "We're just friends. Maybe more, at some point."

"Gordy told me what happened." Dex looked at her.

"What happened? When?" Gloria noticed that Gordy had turned on the TV and his eyes were glued to it.

"About the kissing." Dex wouldn't meet his mother's eyes, clearly embarrassed.

Gloria groaned inwardly. How did parents talk about this with kids? What did a parent say? *Well, kids, you know, how do you think you were born?* Kids didn't want to hear things like that.

"Boys, I'm your mom, but I'm also a grown woman."

"Grown women don't kiss under porch lights." Gordy said, his eyes burning with anger at her.

"I'm sorry, Gordy. I didn't mean for that to happen. I promise that won't happen again."

"And that wasn't the only time. Remember at the festival?" Gordy got up to leave the table. "Forget it. I shouldn't have brought it up."

"Don't go, son. I'm glad you did. We need to talk about this because it's bothering you. What bothers you upsets me. We're a family. We always talk about everything. This is no exception."

"What's going to happen with Matt, Mom?" Dex asked, his head lowered, not looking at her.

"Dex, sweetheart, no matter what happens, please know that I will always love you. You and Gordy will always come first with me. As his daughters will with Matt. But we met and we like each other and we want to see where that takes us. Always remember, too, that no man will ever replace your dad. You know that, don't you?"

"I guess I needed to be reminded," Dex said.

Gloria knew he held a special place in his heart for his dad. Her oldest son remembered when he lived with them. With their divorce, Dex's comfortable world had been shattered.

"Gordy?" Gloria turned to her son, who turned to look at his brother.

"It's okay, Mom. I guess I just needed to hear the words, too."

"All right." Gloria stood up. "Come on. Group hug."

"You're so corny, Mom," Gordy said.

"Yes, I know and you know you love me for it."

The boys joined her in a group hug, her sons' arms around her and around each other. Then, Gordy stepped on his brother's foot, on purpose, and Dex punched him in the stomach. The group hug was over.

"About Amber's birthday party?" Gloria cleared the table.

"Strangers again," Gordy said.

"Only Matt and his girls will be there. It's a family party," Gloria assured them.

"Why are we invited then?" Gordy wondered.

"Because, Matt and I want to do this together."

"This is getting weird, Mom." Dex said.

Gordy didn't say a word, so she knew he agreed with his brother, then with a grin, "Is he going to talk to us about how education is important?"

Dex had a wide smile on his face as well and mimicked Matt's words about education at the barbecue.

"Don't be mean, boys. He was just trying to make conversation."

"Pretty lame," Dex said.

"Let's see what he talks about at his daughter's birthday party, wuss, then we can make fun of him later," Gordy suggested. Both went to their room guffawing.

Gloria smiled in spite of herself and finished clearing up, putting the sandwich fixings in the refrigerator. She did tend to agree with her sons, though. It was weird to talk about another man and his family as part of their lives. *This will be good for all of us*, Gloria thought. She wanted Matt in her life and that meant his family of three daughters. *Oh dear*. Thankfully, his seven siblings weren't going to be there.

Chapter Ten

Gloria drove into the parking lot of the Metro Hospital. Inside this building, on the eighth floor, was the Imaging Center where the EKG would be done. For a woman who enjoyed good health, this made her stop and think. Many women told her of various procedures, tests and surgeries they had endured. Up to this point, the only times she walked into the hospital were when her boys were born. Inside the building, she walked to the elevator bank and pushed the *up* button.

Gloria signed in on the log at the front desk. The receptionist wore black and had small earrings on her right eyebrow. She picked the clipboard up and yelled, "Hey, tell Melinda her eleven o'clock is here! Can I see your insurance and picture I.D.?"

Gloria handed her the cards.

"Fill this form out," the girl said, and pushed back her chair. "Melinda! Man! Josie, I told you to tell her not to leave."

Gloria settled in a chair, hoping that she wouldn't be here forever. She was on her lunch hour after all. Through the years, she had filled out so many forms, for both herself and her sons, at doctor's offices and schools. While looking for a job, she had also completed a lot of applications. Filling out forms came easy for her. She never understood why people found it so difficult. The loud girl at the front desk raised an eyebrow when she handed her the finished paperwork. She looked at it closely, but apparently seemed satisfied with it.

"Someone will be with you shortly."

Gloria sat back down. Why was she thinking about the ease of filling out forms? Her hand clutched her purse strap. She wanted this test over with. But then, what if the EKG showed something abnormal? What would she do then?

"Mrs. Amaya?" A petite girl in light blue scrubs, the

93

uniform of the medical profession, stood at the open door leading into the back offices.

Gloria stood and walked quickly toward the door.

"My name is Melinda. Follow me."

The girl led her down a hall and then right into another one and then into a room with an examining table.

"Here's a gown. Take off your clothes from the waist up, except for your bra. I'll be right back."

Gloria threw her purse on a nearby chair. Pictures of the heart were on the wall. Metal and wood cabinets filled one side of the room. A sink and cabinet were adjacent to the cabinets. She saw the paper towel dispenser and a small pump of hand sanitizer. The nurses at Home Nursing used that to wash their hands when the patients' bathrooms were not clean. Gloria shook her head. She needed to have this test done. Unlike what her dad believed, she'd rather know what was wrong. Gloria climbed up onto the table.

"Ready?" Melinda knocked on the door and peeked in.

"Yes." Gloria swung her legs.

"Lay back." The tech put stickers on her chest and lower legs and applied the wires from the EKG machines, she supposed, to them. Then, she went to the machine and pushed some buttons. A paper spit out from the machine. The tech tore it off, looked at it, then put it in Gloria's chart.

"We're through." The tech removed the stickers and wires.

"Pretty painless," Gloria sighed.

"Yes, it doesn't hurt."

"What are the results?" Gloria knew she wouldn't get an answer.

"Doctor will tell you. You can get dressed and go up to his office. We'll send the results right up." Melinda left.

Gloria pulled the gown together and sat up. Quickly, she dressed and walked to the doctor's office. She signed in and the nurse called her in almost immediately. She sat in a chair in the examining room and looked at another picture of the heart. *Please let my heart be normal.* What if it wasn't? She wanted to at least have one more great sexual encounter before she died. Oh, my!

Why was she thinking like that? And why did the image of Matt's face come to her mind?

"Hi, Gloria." Dr. DeLeon walked in. "How are you feeling?"

Gloria felt her face redden. *Feeling? Wanton, that's how I feel. In a doctor's office thinking of having sex after just having been attached to a heart machine. I am sick—in the head.*

"I'm fine," Gloria muttered.

"Not feeling quite the thing?" Her doctor opened her chart. "You've lost a little bit of weight. Keep that up. Your BP is normal."

"What about the EKG?" Gloria wanted to know.

"Normal."

Gloria heaved a sigh of relief.

"So, we'll continue to monitor your meds. Let me know of any other side effects and keep doing what you're doing. It's working."

"Dr. DeLeon? Last weekend, I tripped and fell and felt dizziness and a ringing in my ears. What was that?"

"Did it last for more than one hour?" The doctor's face creased in concern.

"No, I just couldn't shake it off for a few minutes."

Dr. DeLeon smiled. "As long as it didn't last too long, then you're fine. That happens when we get older. Sudden falls like that can cause dizziness and ringing in your ears due to the fine hairs inside your ears. You'll be fine. See me in six weeks. Take care of yourself."

"Thank you, Doctor." She told him, as he left the room so she could change. Gloria climbed down from the table and muttered, "Now, I can't even fall like I used to."

****

"Come in." Matt opened his front door. "Hello, boys. Glad you came. Go on inside and ask the girls for something to drink." Matt leaned down to kiss Gloria, who turned her head, remembering Gordy's reaction.

"What?" Matt's forehead crinkled in puzzlement.

"Not with the kids around." Gloria walked past Matt and heard the door close behind her.

He walked into the living room and clapped his hands once. "Okay, let's get this party started."

"Happy Birthday, Amber." Gloria hugged the girl and

handed her a pink gift bag.

"More presents!" Amber exclaimed. "I love my birthday."

Julia, for once, seemed happy around her sister. Gloria noticed that Gordy stayed as far away from her as possible, though.

"Are you hungry, guys? I have hot dogs and burgers. Which one for you?"

Her sons followed Matt to the kitchen.

"Can I help with anything?" Gloria offered.

"No, my Dad has everything under control." Julia walked to the stereo and turned the music up loud.

"Julia, turn that down." Matt returned from the kitchen, Dex and Gordy followed. Julia lowered the volume.

Gloria got a paper plate from the table and went to the kitchen. Grilled burgers and wieners were in an aluminum pan topped with foil to keep them warm on top of the stove.

"Help yourself." Matt entered the kitchen. "Sorry about that. I had a talk with the girls, but they still don't understand, especially Julia."

"Understand?" Gloria took her burger to the counter where Matt set up condiments—mustard, mayonnaise, ketchup and lettuce, tomato and onion.

"About us."

"Us." Gloria spread mustard on the hamburger bun.

"Is there an 'us'?" Matt stood near her and she could feel the heat from his body and smell the spicy scent of his cologne mixed in with smoke from the barbecue grill and his own male scent.

"I hope so, but it's so hard." Gloria piled on lettuce and a couple of tomatoes on her burger.

"You've said that before and I agree. But, what do we do? End it because our kids don't like it?" Matt began to fix his own burger.

"We shouldn't let them dictate to us." Gloria sliced her burger in half. "There's degrees of dislike."

"What?" Matt leaned in to kiss her again.

And she wanted to kiss him, but she couldn't. Not with Gordy in the next room as well as Matt's daughters.

"What's the matter with you?" Matt walked to the

refrigerator and pulled out some sodas.

"I had a talk with the boys," Gloria began.

"Oh, you had a talk with the boys." He mimicked.

"Gordy is still very disturbed about catching us kissing." Gloria raised her voice a bit.

"Gloria, that's what couples do. He's seventeen. Don't you think it's time he grew up?" Matt's voice also rose in volume.

"Shh. They'll hear us arguing." Gloria put her finger to her mouth.

"Shit." Matt popped open the sodas.

"And I don't think you should insult my son." Gloria took a deep breath. She wasn't going to get angry. That wouldn't solve anything. Besides, Matt felt the same frustration and confusion she did. "Dex seems okay with you in my life. He was only worried about someone replacing his dad, but I reassured him about that."

"Amber adores you. She keeps telling me you helped her tremendously. Patsy may be a bit confused. Julia, though, she's totally against it. I might as well tell you. She didn't want you or the boys to come."

"That has to do with the argument she had with Gordy. They need to take care of that tonight. Gordy and I already talked about it."

Matt put his arms around Gloria's waist and brought her close to him. She smelled his scent and felt the strength and warmth of his body and leaned into him.

"Let me at least give you a hug. No one can object to a hug, can they?" Matt kissed the top of her head causing shivers up and down her limbs.

"I sure can't." Gloria lifted her lips to his neck, but hearing a noise she quickly backed away.

Julia walked in. "Amber spilled her soda. Where's the carpet cleaner?"

While Matt went to help Julia clean up the spill, Gloria walked to the table and sat down to eat. Her sons had finished eating and were watching TV. Patsy sat near them and talked to Dex. Gordy kept his eyes on the TV.

Her sons pronounced the burgers and hot dogs a hit. Gloria managed to stay away from the chips.

"Time for birthday cake," Matt announced, bringing in the cake to the table.

Gloria marveled at it, decorated with a teenager's theme—little plastic CDs, cell-phones and makeup were featured on the top of the white cake. Yellow icing spelled out *Happy Birthday Amber*.

Matt lit the candles. Gloria waved her sons over to sing to Amber. After the birthday song, Amber blew out the candles and Gloria started the clapping.

"Oh!" Amber exclaimed. "I don't want to cut this pretty cake."

"Do you have a camera?" Gloria asked Matt. "Take a picture, then you can have it forever."

"Great idea! Let me go get the camera," Matt said.

Once Matt took the picture, Amber cut the cake and her proud dad took a picture of that, too. Gloria cut the rest of the cake and served slices to everyone.

"Where's the ice cream?" Amber shouted.

"I'll get it." Patsy ran to the kitchen. "I want some, too."

Gloria's sons stood to one side, eating cake.

"Sit down, boys," Matt invited.

Walking slowly, they sat at the table.

Gloria cut a tiny piece of cake for herself. Just to taste.

"Can I open my presents now?" Amber jumped up and down in her chair.

"Sure, baby." Matt looked at the messy table. "Let's go to the sofa."

"I'm not a baby, Daddy. I'm thirteen," Amber corrected her father.

"Oh, right." Matt grinned.

As Amber opened her presents, Matt continued to take pictures. As usual for kids nowadays, Gloria saw that Amber received quite a collection of CD's and DVD's.

"What kind of music do you boys like?" Matt asked.

Dex stared, then said, "Rap."

Gloria wondered if he thought to scandalize Matt.

"Some of it's pretty good," Matt answered. "That guy on the TV show, 'Fresh Prince'. He's okay."

Gordy groaned.

"What?"

Patsy shook her head at her dad. "That's so old school. Nobody listens to him anymore."

"Oh, Julia." Amber hugged one of the DVD's. "I didn't think you would get me this one. You said only babies watched it."

"They do, you dork. But, you like it so I got it for you."

Amber took the gift bag Gloria had brought.

"I hope you like it, Amber."

"I know I will." Amber took out the pink tissue paper and saw a bottle of perfume. "Oh, yes! I wanted this perfume." She tore the packaging away and opened the bottle and sprayed herself. Getting up from the chair, she ran to Gloria and hugged her. "Thank you."

"You're welcome, honey."

"You put too much perfume on yourself already. You make the whole house smell like you," Julia complained.

"That's a nice perfume, though," Patsy said.

Julia left the room and went out the back door. Gloria was happy Amber had finished opening her presents. How could she reach Julia? Would she ever accept her? Gloria began picking up the discarded wrapping paper. Matt brought a trash bag. She saw Amber admiring her gifts with Patsy. Dex watched T.V. Where had Gordy gone?

"Made it through that," Matt commented as he balled up a paper and threw some bows away.

"Yes, we did," Gloria sighed.

"Should we do it again?" Matt walked to the kitchen with the trash bag.

"Maybe in a couple of years." Gloria looked out the window and saw Julia and Gordy. "What are they doing out there? I hope they don't argue again."

Matt pushed the curtain aside to see better.

"Don't!" Gloria closed the curtain. "We don't want them to think we're spying."

"We are," Matt grinned.

"No, we're not. I just hope things don't get worse."

Gloria helped Matt clean up the table and the kitchen. Patsy and Amber helped by throwing away used paper plates.

"I want to see you tomorrow. The girls will be back with Angela. I'm taking them back tonight. What do you say?" Matt pulled her into his arms.

"I'd like that. What shall we do?"

"Let's go to a restaurant where it's quiet and there are no kids around," Matt suggested.

"Sounds like a plan." Gloria buried her face in Matt's neck.

"Mom."

"Dad."

Gloria stepped away quickly from Matt. Gordy and Julia stood at the doorway of the kitchen.

"We want to talk to you," Julia said, coming inside the kitchen and standing near her dad.

Gloria's heart moved and lodged in her throat. What now?

"I apologized to her," Gordy said.

"Did you mean it, son?" Gloria asked.

"Yes, he was very nice about it." Julia glanced quickly at Gordy, then back at her dad, then at Gloria, her eyes huge.

"I'm sorry about putting your present to Amber down. She loves that perfume. Lately, she loves any perfume. But, at least, the one you gave her smells nice." Julia looked at Gloria, then at the floor and put her hands in her back pockets. "Dad, I'll try to understand about you and—Gloria."

Matt hugged his daughter. "That's all I ask, sweetheart."

Julia left the kitchen.

Gordy held out his hand to Matt. "I'm sorry I was rude, sir."

Matt looked at Gloria, then took Gordy's hand. "Apology accepted, Gordy. Your mom is a special lady. I think I'd be the same way if I were you."

Gordy nodded at Gloria. Before he left the room, she blew him a kiss and whispered, "Thank you, sweetie."

"What do you think about that?" Matt pulled Gloria back into his arms.

"I think maybe we can have another birthday party in a year now." Gloria laughed.

****

Once home, after the afternoon at Matt's, Dex and Gordy had gone to the video store to rent some games. Gloria sat on the textured brown and white sofa and read a book, a romance by a new author and so far very enjoyable. Engrossed in the story, she didn't hear the doorbell right away and actually thought it was the T.V. She liked to keep the set on when alone.

She stood and walked toward the front door. Who could it be at this hour? Her heart lifted in her chest. Was it Matt? He would have called first. Looking through the peephole, she thought she could be hallucinating. Eddie Amaya stood outside. What was he doing here? Gloria looked at her clothes—jeans, T-shirt. Her hands flew to her hair. A mess, as usual. And she probably needed to dye it again.

The doorbell pealed again, followed by several knocks on the door.

Taking a deep breath, Gloria opened the door.

"It's about time." Her ex-husband stated, not even with a greeting or a smile. Wasn't that just like him though?

"What are you doing here?" He stood there, tall and lean, his black hair had a few gray streaks in it. However, blast it, on him the gray looked good, not as if he were getting old as it looked on her.

"Is that any way to greet your loving ex?" He had the audacity to grin.

"Eddie, I'd describe you in many ways, but 'loving' isn't one of them."

"Yes, Dex told me you're dating." Eddie entered her home without asking. She moved out of the way because he made a move to hug her. "What's up with that?"

"You sound like Gordy. But he's a teenager."

"Now, you don't like how I talk."

The typical scene with Eddie. They could argue about anything—even the color of the sky. She sighed.

"Did you come here to pick a fight with me?"

Eddie shrugged and walked around the living room, looking at the pictures. "No pictures of Matt?"

"I'm not going to talk to you about him. It's none of your business."

"Of course, it is. He's coming into the house where my sons live."

Gloria had to laugh at that. His sons, were they? Where had he been during her struggle to keep food on

101

the table and a sane mind?

Eddie glared as she continued laughing. "Pull yourself together, Gloria."

"Oh Eddie. You're always good for a laugh—or an argument. Again, I ask you. What are you doing here?"

"I came to see my sons. Just wondering what's going on with them now that you're allowing another man around you. Have you been to bed with him?" Eddie's nostrils flared.

Why so angry? They weren't married anymore, hadn't been for several years. And at least she had waited until the divorce before doing so. Damn him for making her feel as if she had to justify her actions.

"Look, Eddie. What I'm doing is no concern of yours. It hasn't been for a long time now. You have a right to see your sons, but not in my home. You've never done this before."

"You've never dated before."

"Yes, I have. You just haven't known about it because it's never been long term." She retorted and wondered why she had spoken of a permanent relationship. Did she really want that?

"Is this for real?" Eddie frowned, his eyes flickered from her to the pictures on the mantel.

Her ex leaned close to her. She could smell his cologne, fresh—like a cool breeze blowing on her and filling her nostrils. Gloria backed away from him. She had no feelings for him anymore. He was just her sons' father.

"I don't know. It's too new."

"Gloria, Gloria. You know you'll never replace me." He smirked.

"I'm not trying to replace you."

"Then, why haven't you ever found someone else?"

"Because I'm pickier than you are." She snapped back.

"Yeah, I've had like four or five women in the last few years."

Gloria sniffed and said, "More like ten or twelve, I would venture to guess."

Eddie laughed, his eyes lighting up in merriment. The sight took her back to the good times when they'd been alone after Dex was asleep.

"You have no shame, Eddie Amaya."

"Don't marry him, Gloria."

"What?" She stared at her ex. "What do you mean? Besides, the subject hasn't even come up. How dare you tell me what to do?"

The front door swung open. Her sons were home. Dex was the first one in. He threw the plastic bag from the video store on the nearest chair and greeted his dad. "Hey, Dad. You didn't tell me you were coming. Did you? I'm sorry I forgot if you did."

"No, Dex. I didn't tell you. Just wanted to come visit with your mom a little bit before we go somewhere. Have ya'll eaten?"

"Hi, Dad." Gordy hugged his dad with only one arm and patted his back a little. Her youngest son wasn't as close to his dad as Dex. It bothered Dex more than it seemed to bother Eddie. He really didn't even know Gordy.

"Of course, they have, Eddie. It's almost eleven at night." Gloria said, still angry that Eddie had arrived without notice and begun ordering her around.

"Mom, is something wrong?" Dex asked, his eyes huge in his face, reminding her of when he'd been a little boy and he would try to be peacemaker between his arguing parents.

"No, *mijo*." Gloria put her arm around Dex. "There's nothing wrong. Your dad just surprised me by coming over. That's all. He usually calls."

"I had to make an emergency visit this time. Your mom is dating." Eddie stuffed his hands in his jeans.

Dex looked upset. Gloria knew he regretted telling his dad anything about Matt.

"I just told him a visit wasn't necessary." She reassured her son.

"Let's go somewhere, Dad." Dex said. "Mom is probably ready to go to bed. Right, Mom? Gordy and I'll go with you to get a soda or something."

Gordy agreed, but looked as if he wanted to say no.

"Go to bed and dream of your new man?" Eddie taunted.

"Come on, Dad." Dex led his father toward the front door.

"We need to talk more about this, Gloria." Eddie told her as he left.

Gloria shut the door. Dex and Gordy said they'd be right back. She leaned against the door for a few seconds. What was the matter with Eddie? Did he really think she'd stay single forever? Like some trophy that's stored away and forgotten? She had a right to live her life and if that included a man, then it would and he had no right to tell her what to do. Who did he think he was, anyway? The smell of his cologne lingered in the room. Memories clouded her mind. She had loved Eddie, so much that she eloped with him. That part of her life was over, though. Matt was the new chapter in her life and she liked him, maybe more could develop between them—and there was nothing wrong with that.

Chapter Eleven

Matt ran the lawn mower over the grass. He'd lost another helper, so here he was working again. The outdoors—he loved it. Always had. He'd never forgotten working in the garden with his mother. Gone too soon. He wiped his face with a rag. Mornings in San Antonio in the summer tended to be scorchers as well. This morning, however, was kinda cool, but working in yards made him sweat no matter what the weather. Maybe it would rain. The sky did look a bit cloudy. He and Gloria were going out—somewhere. He hadn't decided where. Maybe she had an idea. He knew he'd rather spend it at his house— alone with her. But, he had promised her a restaurant.

The ringing of his cell interrupted his thoughts. "Matt, darling, I need you."

Angela. What did she want now? He stopped the lawn mower and walked to the truck to get a drink of water. "I'm not lending you any more money," Matt said before she could say another word. And took a drink of the cold water from the jug he always carried.

"I don't want money. It's something more," Angela wailed.

"Is something wrong with the girls?" Matt had just seen them last night, but anything could happen in a matter of minutes. He felt chilled at the thought they might be in danger.

"The girls?" Angela sounded flustered. "No, nothing's the matter with the girls. It's me, you idiot. I have the problem."

"I'm in the middle of a job. In other words, I'm busy. Can't this wait?"

"You're never available anymore. You're always with that bimbo."

"Please don't call her names. She's a woman and a mother of two sons. She's not a bimbo."

"Right. She's dating a married man. What does that

105

make her?"

"I'm not a married man anymore. You saw to that."

"I want you back, Matt."

He heard Angela sniffling. Was she crying?

Matt rolled his eyes. "Don't put on the crying act. What do you want? I know you don't want to be married to me, otherwise you wouldn't have destroyed our family."

"Destroyed our family? How melodramatic you are. If anyone destroyed it, it was you. Always working with weeds. What about your family? When did you take time to remember your family?"

"The girls have never told me that I wasn't around. I've seen them a lot of times in my house and we always have a good time. They don't seem to have any complaints." But her words made him think twice. Had he neglected his girls? At the time Angela asked him for a divorce, she claimed that he neglected her. Jorge, apparently, filled the void in her life.

"That's because you've brainwashed them. They've learned to accept what little you give."

Matt felt the hot sun climbing the sky. "Angela, I've gotta go. I'm on a job like I said. I need to get back to it."

"I need you, Matt. Please come back to me."

"Angela…" He couldn't believe what his ex-wife had said.

"Oh, all right. It's Jorge. He came and wants me back, but I don't want him. Creep! How can he even think that I would consider returning to him after he's been with another woman? It's ludicrous!"

Matt couldn't help pointing the obvious to her. "I don't want you either for the very same reason."

"I just thought if he saw you around, he'd back off. Can you come, Matt? Please? I'll make it worth your while."

"How can you do that? There's nothing I want from you anymore except time to spend with my daughters."

"Thanks a lot, Matt. I can never count on you. First, it was your plants, now it's that damn bimbo." Angela paused. "Does she know about your fear of illness?"

"I don't have a fear of illness," Matt denied.

"Like hell you don't. Remember how you acted every time the girls got sick. And when Patsy had her operation, you were a basket case. Wonder if I should tell your new woman what a coward you are."

Matt knew she was pushing his buttons because he wouldn't help her, but he refused to rise to the bait. "I repeat, I don't have a fear of illness. I just don't like to be around sick people."

Angela laughed. "How old is she? In her forties? I'd be surprised if she doesn't have some disease already. Have you slept with her? Maybe before you do you should suggest she go to the doctor and have herself checked out."

Matt curbed the urge to hang up on his ex. "Where do you come up with these things? I've got to go. Unlike you, I have to work to make a living."

"I work, too. I have the stock kit."

"How much money have you made with it?"

"Well, I haven't really started. There's a lot of information that I have to read before I start the actual work."

"Right." Matt opened the door to the truck. "I've got to go."

"Why don't you believe me anymore?" Angela whined.

"Maybe because I don't trust you anymore."

And she hung up on him. Matt flung the cell to the seat. Finally, he had riled her enough for her to hang up. He remembered her barb about his fear of sickness. She was wrong about that. The girls had been sick a lot during the time he and Angela were together. Kids got sick. He knew that. His dad was getting older and he was bound to get sick, too. His stomach lurched at the thought but he put that down to the tacos he had eaten for breakfast not the fact that he was afraid his dad would become ill. Of course, he didn't want his dad to be sick, or his daughters, or anyone else he cared about. Everyone felt that way. That didn't mean he harbored some kind of phobia about illness the way Angela had insinuated.

He stepped out of the truck. His ex—all she had ever been good for was to make him second guess himself. No, he had his daughters because of her. No matter what else happened, Angela would always be the mother of his girls. But, she was wrong. He had no fears or phobias—of that he was positive.

****

"Mom, I found the perfect ride," Dex announced, peering into the shed.

Gloria was on the treadmill, breathing hard. She had increased the incline, but she was about to lower it. It was too much for her. Her calves were burning. With a few taps, she lowered the incline and slowed the rate. Gloria saw her son and pulled off the earphones to her CD player. "What did you say, Dex?"

"It's an SUV."

"An SUV? What about it?"

"I want to buy it," Dex grinned.

"Oh Dex, I thought you were going to buy a smaller vehicle. Do you know how much gas those things use?"

"This is a good buy. It's a 2000 model, AC, you know it has to have that, cassette player, you know I want that so I can use my car kit to plug in my MP3 player. It also has a CD player." He enumerated the essentials, at least in his thinking.

"What about the engine, the tires, that unimportant stuff?" Gloria kept walking on the treadmill.

"I took it to a mechanic I know. He said the engine was good. It'll need new tires soon, but other than that, it's in good shape. And I'll have enough money left in my savings to buy tires when I need them. I'm going to go get it so you can see it. I came by to pick up Gordy so he can go with me." Dex left with another grin.

Gloria turned off the treadmill. She wiped the sweat with a rag. Climbing onto the exercise bicycle, she put the earphones back on and pedaled the bicycle. She closed her eyes to listen to seventies music. And to think about Dex and the SUV. She supposed she'd have to let him get the SUV if it really turned out to be in good condition. She couldn't spend the rest of her days looking over his shoulder. Dex would rebel at that, she knew.

"Mom, tell that—Matt person—to mind his own business." Dex handed the cordless phone to her and walked away.

This time she heard him through her music. He yelled. What had upset him? She put the phone to her ear.

"Hello?"

Matt's voice came over the line. "I made your son

mad. Just when everything had been cleared up." He sighed.

"What did Dex say to you?"

"It's more like what I said to him. He told me about the SUV he found. Sounded very excited about it. Instead of being happy for him, I acted like a parent, step-parent I should say, and cautioned him about the gas guzzlers they can be."

"Oh no. I just told him the same thing." Gloria stopped peddling the bicycle. "He'll get over it, Matt. He's on his way to get it so I can see it."

"Was it this hard for our parents, you think?"

"I'm sure it was." Gloria wiped her face again.

"Man. No wonder some people prefer not to have kids."

"Once you have them, though, you can't give them back and you don't want to." Gloria smiled as she remembered her sons as babies.

"Yeah, you're right about that." She heard Matt's sigh again. "I won't say another word about his truck. So, are we going out tonight?" His tone changed from a concerned parent to a seductive man asking his woman out.

Gloria's body trembled with anticipation. "I'm looking forward to it. Where are we going?"

"There's a restaurant someone told me about near downtown. It's quiet, none of that loud tourist stuff."

"Sounds great." Gloria stopped pedaling the bicycle.

"It's not too far from the River Walk, either. We can go if there's not too many people. What do you say?"

"I'd love it. What time?"

"Seven."

"I'll be waiting."

Gloria hung up and sat still on the exercise bicycle as she thought about Matt and the evening with him. Slowly, she started pedaling again. She couldn't wait.

****

When Gloria slid the patio door open and stepped inside, she found Dex lying on the sofa, dazedly flipping the channels on the TV. "What's the matter?"

"The SUV."

Gordy walked in from the kitchen, a bottle of water

109

in his hand. "The man sold it before we got there. He had another one, but it was yellow."

Gloria laughed. "Yellow's not so bad. Besides, you could always paint it."

"This was a weird yellow, like mustard-colored. It had dents and a big crack in the windshield." Dex threw the remote on the coffee table. "I'll never find a good truck."

"You will." She sat on the armchair diagonally from her oldest son. "Of course, I'd prefer if you'd get a car. It'll save you on gas."

"Mom, at this point in my life, I don't want to save on gas. I want a nice truck." Dex sat up. "And why did you have to tell Matt about my business?"

"I didn't tell him anything. You did."

"Tell him to stay out of my life." Dex stomped out of the room.

Gordy looked at Gloria. "He's just upset. All the way to the place he talked about the SUV, then when he saw it, it was a piece of—"

"Gordy." Her tone warned him not to say what he was thinking.

"Uh...it was beat up." Her son grinned.

"Nice recovery." She stood up and looked at her watch. "I need to get ready. Matt will be here in an hour or so."

"I'm going to my room. I don't have to come out and say hello, do I?"

"I'm not going to do it." Dex yelled from his room.

"It would be nice for my sons to be sociable with the man I—" Gloria stopped. Her heart went up to her throat. What was she about to say?

"Mom." Gordy's voice mimicked her warning tone of before.

"With the man I'm dating."

"Nice recovery." Her son finished the bottle of water. "I think."

Gloria went to her room to decide what she should wear tonight. And think about what she had been about to say. She didn't love Matt, did she? No, she didn't. It was too soon. She was just going out with a nice man for an evening. That's all. Period. End of story.

****

"Mom, I have to talk to you." Gordy almost toppled her as she stepped out of the bathroom where she had been taking a shower.

"What? You almost pushed me down, son." Gloria fluffed her hair with the towel to dry it.

"I'm going out tonight," Gordy grinned.

"Who are you going with? Will?"

"No." Her son lowered his eyes to the floor. "A girl."

Gloria stopped fluffing her hair. "A girl? When did you make this date?"

"Just now. She called me."

"She called you?" She continued drying her hair with the towel. "Things are so different nowadays. In my day girls didn't call boys."

Gordy looked at her with that expression she had noticed when he was a baby, as if she was making a big deal out of nothing.

"Okay. When, where, how, who? Tell me all the details."

"She'll be going to my school. I met her at work. She's a new girl at the print shop."

"What's her name?"

"Cassie."

"Let's go sit down," Gloria said, as they were still standing in front of the bathroom.

Gordy sat on the armchair in the living room, one leg over one of the sides.

"She's going to college, too, she said." Gordy's lip curled.

"You don't believe her?" Gloria sat on the sofa.

"Whatever." Her son flipped the channels on the T.V.

"Do you really like this girl, son? Or, are you up to something?" Gloria didn't like her son's attitude.

"I already went out with her a couple of times. Well, not actually out. Just to this place near work."

"Why hadn't you told me before?"

"It's not important."

"So you're just playing with this girl."

"That's what girls do, Mom, so why shouldn't I do it?"

"Because that's not the values I taught you, young man. I suggest you don't go out with her unless you're sincere. Gordy, a relationship is not worth anything if you're not truthful." Gloria's stomach did flip-flops as she remembered that she hadn't been totally honest with Matt.

"Aw, Mom! It's all in fun."

"Have you forgotten how you felt when Kayla dumped you? What if Cassie really falls for you? You're going to hurt her. Don't do things like that, son. That's not how I brought you up."

"Should I break the date, then? She's already waiting for me. She just rang to tell me she was ready."

"Well, I guess not. That would be mean, to break it off at the last minute. You need to tell her the truth tonight."

"Just come right out and say that I don't like her that much after all?"

"Gordy, you have to be nice. I know you know how to do that."

"I thought you'd be happy I was going out with girls again," Gordy huffed.

"I am, son, if you're happy. But, I don't think you are. You're pretending to be a—what's that word you boys use?"

"Player?" Her son muttered.

"Yes. And you're not that way."

"How do you know?"

"Because I'm your mother." Gloria flicked him with the towel.

Gordy yelled and jumped up from the chair to get out of the way. "Are you going out tonight?"

"Yes, Matt and I are going downtown. Okay with you?"

"I'm glad you're asking for my permission." Gordy grinned and teasing, he said, "And, no, it's not okay."

Gloria grabbed him and gave him a tight hug, "Well, too bad, I'm going anyway."

As Gordy went to his room, Gloria decided that she'd tell Matt the truth about her health tonight. She had advised her son to be truthful and she had to practice what she preached.

****

"You look gorgeous." Matt looked her up and down

when she opened the door.

"It only took me all day to look this way." Gloria looked down at herself. She had just put navy blue pants on and a nice blouse, but seeing Matt's eyes she felt as if she was wearing an evening gown and tiara.

"Worth every minute it took." Matt leaned in to kiss her, then looked behind her and all around her. "Are your sons home? Can I sneak in a kiss, or two?"

Gloria laughed. "Dex is riding around with his friend. And Gordy had a date."

"I thought he had sworn off girls."

"He had. And he's not really over Kayla. He's just playing with this girl and I advised him to put an end to that tonight."

"You girls do it to us guys, see? Even a nice boy like your son turns mean at the first contact with girls." Matt put his finger to his mouth and tapped it.

"It works both ways, Mister. I haven't had the best experience with you men."

Matt laughed and pulled her into his arms. "That has now changed." Bending his head, he kissed her lightly on the lips.

Gloria regretted the quick kiss and tried to prolong it.

He pushed her away gently, "If you do that, we'll never leave."

"That might not be a bad idea." Gloria kept her arms around his waist.

"I'll hold you to that. For now, I've made reservations at a very elegant place."

"Should I have worn a dress?" Gloria wrinkled her brow.

"No, you're fine. Just a figure of speech." Matt took her hand. "Let's go."

Once downtown, Matt parked at a nearby parking garage. The night was not blistering hot. At least she could breathe without feeling as if she was swallowing hot air.

"It's a few blocks down from here. Ready for a walk?"

Gloria saw a horse and buggy going by. "Can't we take that? I already did my walking on the treadmill today."

"I wasn't with you, though." Matt put his arm around her waist and she leaned into him.

"Oh yes. This does feel much better."

Matt kissed her lightly on the lips again. Anticipation made her tremble. Gloria hated to ruin the evening by bringing up her health issues. High blood pressure wasn't that big of a deal. Besides, she was on medication and for the most part, she felt fine. Why was she hesitant to tell Matt? For one thing, the thought of having hypertension made her feel old, probably due to the fact that she saw this type of diagnosis at work all the time. And usually, the person diagnosed was elderly. But, she also noticed a stiffening of Matt's body whenever sickness was mentioned. Why was that? What if he were one of those people who couldn't stand illness? Well, actually nobody could, but some people had practically a phobia about it.

Gloria walked along with Matt thinking these thoughts. She followed him down some concrete stairs to the River Walk, the famous tourist attraction of San Antonio. The San Antonio River had actually been very useful to the early settlers for domestic and transporting reasons.

"Doesn't look too crowded yet." Matt led her through a narrow opening where a group of people waited to enter an Irish pub.

"Do you know that for St. Patrick's Day the city dyes the water green?"

Matt nodded.

"Have you ever seen it green?" Gloria looked at the river flowing quietly between concrete and clubs and restaurants along both sides. Trees on either side almost formed a canopy over it.

"When I was little. Dad would bring us down here. He wanted to make sure they hadn't put too much dye in and killed the fish. Everyone would assure him the dye was harmless, but he didn't believe them." Matt laughed in remembrance. "I've got to take you to meet him soon."

Gloria nodded, then because the thought of meeting his dad and what that signified flustered her, she leaned her body against his and asked, "Which restaurant are we going to?"

"It's called Little Italia. I hear they've got the best spaghetti."

Gloria panicked. She couldn't eat spaghetti in front of Matt. She could just see herself flicking spaghetti sauce all over the place and maybe even on Matt. She'd order a salad.

Once they'd arrived, the hostess led them to a small table for two situated in a dimly lit corner. Soft piano music rippled through the restaurant. In the center of the table a candle stood flickering. "Your server will be right with you."

"This is nice." Gloria hung her purse on a wooden chair, which gleamed.

"What may I get you to drink? Would you like to see the wine list?" The young girl in black top and pants and a small white apron asked with a smile.

"Gloria?" Matt asked.

"No, I'll just have some iced water with lemon."

Matt nodded. "I'll have some red wine. Thanks."

Gloria looked around, but her eyes settled on Matt across the table from her. His eyes looked even darker in the candlelight and mesmerized her. It would be so easy to fall into his arms tonight and stay there.

"Do you like this place?"

"Yes. Very good choice. Have you ever been here before?" Gloria hoped not.

"I haven't brought anyone else here," Matt grinned.

"Good," Gloria said quickly. "I mean, how did you find it?"

"One of my workers told me about it. He recently met a girl and wanted to impress her, so he brought her here."

The waitress arrived with their drinks. "Are you ready to order, or do you want more time?"

Gloria realized she hadn't even looked at the menu. She picked up the glossy red card.

"Give us a few minutes," Matt told the waitress.

"What do you recommend? Oh, you said the spaghetti," Gloria remembered.

"That's what I'm getting." Matt sipped his wine.

Opening the menu, she saw the menu items written in gold script and no prices, a sure sign that everything was expensive. This was a restaurant that catered to people who didn't care how much dinner cost. "Did you say one of your workers recommended this restaurant to you? You must pay them very well."

"No, the poor sap used practically a whole paycheck and the evening was a disaster." Matt gave her a sheepish grin and scratched his hand. "I'm not trying to impress you, Gloria. Well, maybe a little. I mainly brought you here because it's quiet and we can be alone."

"What a wonderful thought. I'll just order a salad, though, I'm not very hungry."

When the waitress returned, that's what she did.

"I have something to tell you." Gloria took a sip of water.

"This sounds serious," Matt winked at her.

She squirmed in her chair, crossed her legs. Matt watched her.

"Is it that serious?"

I have high blood pressure. Gloria practiced the words inside her head, but when she actually voiced it, she said, "I...I'm looking for another job."

Matt waited, took the wine goblet in his hand.

"I told you I was tired of being in home health, didn't I? Well, I've sent out some resumes and applied at a couple of bookstores. So far, I haven't heard anything, but I'm keeping my fingers crossed."

"That's good." Matt stared at her.

"What?" Gloria picked up her glass of water and drank.

"It's just that, well, it seemed as if you were going to say something else. Changing jobs is serious, but, forget it. The girls always tell me that I overanalyze."

Gloria looked down at the flickering candle in the middle of the table. *Yes, Matt, I want to tell you something else, but I can't bring myself to do it. Why?* She looked up and was about to try again when the food arrived.

Matt rubbed his hands together. "This does smell like the best spaghetti in town."

The waitress smiled. "Good choice, sir." She put down the plate with Gloria's salad—mixed greens and romaine lettuce. "Can I get you anything else? More wine?"

"This is fine. I will have a glass of water, please." Matt said.

"Very good, sir. Enjoy your meal."

Gloria forked up some salad and tasted it.

"Do you want to try the spaghetti?" Matt offered.

She looked at his beautiful brown eyes and wanted to jump into their depths and drown in them. But, she was being dishonest and she couldn't make herself tell him the truth.

"Sure." She twirled a little bit of spaghetti on her fork. "Ummm. You're right. It is good. The sauce has a spicy taste, but not too spicy and not to tomato-y. Wonder how they make it."

"Maybe they'll tell us. Though most cooks like to keep their recipes a secret." Matt continued eating.

Gloria's stomach fluttered at the word. *Tell him. If he turns away from you, then you don't need him in your life.* But, why would he? It's not as if she had anything contagious.

By the time, the waitress came for the plates, she and Matt had changed the topic of conversation to the kids. Then, she walked with Matt back to the car. Again, he put his arm around her waist. Walking so close together always bothered her before. But, not with Matt. With him, she just wanted to be as close as possible to him.

In the car, Matt kissed her. She felt his lips on hers and inched up closer.

"Are you enjoying yourself?"

"The food was delicious." Gloria murmured and gave herself up to his kiss. When she could breathe again, she continued, "And the company is so tasty, too."

"Let's go home." Matt turned the ignition.

Chapter Twelve

"Come to my room." He said, once they were inside his house.

"Yes." Gloria allowed him to lead the way. This was what she wanted. Briefly, the image of Eddie intruded. *Don't marry him, Gloria.* But he hadn't even asked.

She felt the warmth of Matt's hand as he led her to his bed. She barely saw her surroundings—brown, green, burgundy—all blended into the man who was awakening her senses again. Eddie was history and Matt was now.

He slowly unbuttoned her blouse, pulled it from her shoulders and let it fall to the floor. Her bra came off next. With his mouth and his hands, he caressed and teased.

"I think there's still too much clothing between us."

"So do I," Gloria said, but didn't want to let him go.

Item by item, she managed to get out of her clothes and so did he.

Feeling self-conscious about her flaws, she almost wanted to grab the covers to hide herself from him, "I don't look like a teenager now, do I?"

"No, you look so much better."

He caressed her stomach, which poofed out more than it should, and around to her hips. She trembled.

"You look so much better." He repeated.

Leaning into her, he inched her down to the bed and followed her. She felt the weight of him on top of her and she welcomed it—his hardness on her softer curves. It made her feel feminine. Something she hadn't felt in years. The soap he had used filled her senses—fresh scent mixed with his spicy cologne and male aroma.

He kissed her for endless minutes, his hand touching her everywhere—neck, breasts and thighs. Her hands caressed his back, hard and smooth at the same time. His body was warm against hers. His hand inched down, past her navel. When he touched her there—in her center, she gasped. Then, her hips moved, wanting release. She wanted Matt inside her.

"Take me now, Matt."

He laughed and the sound made her shiver. He continued to caress her, then she saw him tear at something with his teeth—protection. Not that she would get pregnant, but it was better to be safe nowadays.

"Do you want me to put it on for you?" Gloria asked.

"Not on your life. If you touch me now..."

His body took possession of hers and she gasped.

"Oh yes!"

Moving to the rhythm of the sounds of love, Matt led her to a climax that exploded into a million stars and left her feeling lethargic, but a woman again. Her heart was beating very rapidly. For a brief moment, she feared a stroke. Matt stirred above her, his breath coming fast, too.

Then, he kissed her. His lips were warm, sweet. She felt him inside her and knew she could come again. His body and hers seemed glued together with sweat, warmth and love. Matt moved away from her.

"Where are you going?" The wonderful lethargy suffused her whole body, which seemed as if it were still vibrating with the rhythm of love.

"I'll be right back."

Gloria closed her eyes and could feel her heart rate slowing down. She stretched on the warm sheets and covered herself up to her head. The happiness she felt flowed through her veins.

"Hey, where'd you go?" Matt was back.

She flung back the covers and saw Matt by the bed with two glasses of white wine. "Just a sip. To make a toast."

Taking the glass from him, she sat up, holding the sheet to cover herself.

"I wouldn't mind if you let that sheet go," Matt grinned.

"I know, but I would. What are we toasting?"

"To the most beautiful rose princess." Matt clinked his glass with hers.

"To the most beautiful rose gardener." Gloria grinned. "But—remember, *I'm Mary, Mary.*"

Matt joined her under the sheets and grabbed her around the waist. "Not to me." He kissed her.

She sighed and closed her eyes, one arm around him, the other holding her glass of wine.

Matt took it from her, placed both glasses on a nearby table, then moved his body over hers. His mouth covered hers and she put one leg around his to bring him closer.

"I hate to say this." Gloria gasped as she tore her lips from Matt's. "But, I think I'd better go."

"You mean you're not going to stay here with me?" He asked with a pout set to his mouth.

"I wish. But, I can't."

"It's your sons again." Matt still lay on top of her, but buried his head in the pillow.

"Matt..."

"No, I understand, I think." He raised his head and looked at her with his soft brown gaze.

She brought him down to her again and nuzzled his neck. "Do you know that I love how you smell?"

"Even with sweat and dirt on me?"

"Even then. We'll do this again."

"I'm holding you to that." Matt threw the covers back.

Gloria screeched. "No, you meanie!" And tried to cover herself.

Matt's gaze raked her from top to bottom. "Okay, I'll take you home." His hand caressed her from her face down to her neck to one side of her breast to her nipple and stayed there playing with it. "But under protest."

She sighed. "If you don't stop touching me, I may not go home." Gloria's eyes settled on his body, evenly browned by the sun with a muscled chest. So what if he had a few sags here and there. They were of an age, but he still looked so good to her.

"Well, in that case..." Matt began to push her gently to the mattress.

Gloria jumped out of bed, grabbed her clothes and ran to the bathroom.

****

When they arrived at Gloria's house, her sons were still out, thank goodness. She didn't think she could hide what she felt.

"I'll call you tomorrow," Matt said at her door.

Gloria unlocked the door, opened it and reached in

and flicked the porch light off. "I'll hold you to that."

"So, are we going to neck on the porch again?" Matt pulled her into his arms.

"Yes, only this time with no porch light on." Gloria lifted her lips up for his kiss. Still feeling the after effects of their lovemaking, she remembered tomorrow was Sunday. "I'm going to church tomorrow and I bought barbecue plates so we're eating there. I wish you could join us."

"I have a job to do in the morning. But I'll call you." Matt walked away. "And, in the meantime, try to think of what you were going to tell me before when you told me that story about another job."

Gloria stared after him. "You didn't believe me?"

"I'm the father of three girls. I believe that you're looking for another job, but I don't believe that's what you meant to tell me. I've learned to recognize the subtle signs when they're keeping things from me. And I saw that in you." With that he got in his truck and left.

****

Gloria looked at her alarm clock. 8:00 a.m. blazed at her in red. It started the irritating beeping. She hit the snooze button and switched it off. Snuggling inside the sheets, she burrowed her head into her pillow. In her mind's eye, she could still see Matt's naked body as it had been last night. Heck! She could still feel it. "Oh." She dragged out the word and wiggled her legs. After all these years, she had made love—and with what a man. He was not only a great gardener. He was a great lover. She giggled as she wondered if there was a proven correlation on that. What if she googled it? What would the computer's search engine come up with?

"Mom, are you dreaming?" Gordy stood at her bedroom doorway. She never closed her door. When her boys were little, she hated to be so far away from them to begin with as they slept in another room let alone closing her door against them. Besides, they knew to call out before barging in.

"Yes, I am dreaming." Gloria sang the words.

"Oh man! Something's the matter with mom. She woke up singing."

"She had a date last night, remember, Gordo?" Dex

121

said from the living room.

"What are ya'll doing up so early on a Sunday?"

"I want to tell you about my date." Gordy said.

"He wouldn't let me sleep." Dex peeked in the doorway.

"Okay, I'm up. Be right there." Gloria threw off the sheets and pictured Matt flinging the sheets off her last night. It would take awhile for her not to be shy around him about her body. Awhile? He said this wasn't temporary. But, she also remembered she hadn't told him about her high blood pressure. She had to do it today.

She joined her sons at the dining room table. Dex was eating a bowl of cereal, Gordy, waffles.

"Yum. I want some waffles." Gloria inhaled the smell of waffles and syrup, sugary and doughy.

"Here's your breakfast bar, Mom." Gordy handed her the box.

"Oh you." She took it, however, unwrapped it and bit into the multi-grain apple-filled bar. Walking to the sink, she filled her mug with water to make tea.

"So, how was your date?" Gloria asked.

"How was yours?" Both boys asked.

"It was fabulous." She sang the words.

"Forget it, Mom. I don't think we want to know." Dex spooned in some cereal into his mouth.

"We went to the River Walk and strolled, hand in hand, arm in arm."

"Please, Mom." Gordy covered his ears and closed his eyes.

"Then, we ate at a wonderful Italian place on the river, the best spaghetti, at least that's what Matt ate. I only tasted a little bit. I had a salad."

"A salad?" Dex looked at her with eyes wide open. "You're at an Italian restaurant and you order a salad?"

"Lame, Mom, really lame." Gordy placed a dripping piece of waffle in his mouth.

"So, how was your date, son?" Gloria bit into her breakfast bar.

"Well, you know I started out to tell her that I didn't like her as much as I thought. Do you know what she did?"

"What?" Both Dex and Gloria asked.

"She said she didn't like me. She agreed to go out with me so that she could meet Will." Gordy smiled and took another bite of waffle.

"Why do you seem happy, then?" Gloria frowned.

"Because after we came clean, we began to enjoy our time together. She's not so bad. We went to a movie and talked about it afterwards. Got some ice cream."

"I'm happy for you, Gordy." Gloria sipped her tea.

"Yeah, well, I didn't ask her out again."

A phone rang, Gordy's cell phone. He grinned when he looked at the number. "That's her. She can't bear not to hear my voice." He walked away from the table.

"Hey, don't forget, we're going to church. Make the call short."

Gordy nodded at her and left the room.

"What do you think, Dex? I don't want him to get hurt again." Gloria creased her brow.

"You can't stop things like that, Mom. Everybody gets hurt."

"You're right. If we never tried again, we'd never get anywhere. Okay. I'll just keep my fingers crossed and pray. Which reminds me. Let's get ready for church."

"Uh, Mom?" Dex stopped her.

When Gloria turned back to her son, he continued, "Dad called last night. He knows about an SUV I can buy. I'm going to go see it today."

Her heart lurched inside her. Oh Eddie, why was he getting involved in this? He always let Dex down. She just knew something would not be right with this SUV. However, somehow he would convince Dex it was the best buy he could ever make. She had to talk to him.

"Drive it over here. I want to see it before you buy it. And I want to talk to your dad, too."

"Aw, Mom. I can make my own decisions." Dex protested.

"I know you can, son. Most of the time. But not when your dad is involved."

"You and Dad have never agreed on anything. You won't about this SUV. I shouldn't have said anything. I'll never find a truck." Dex stomped to his room.

"Get ready for church. We'll talk about this later."

"I'm through talking." Dex shouted from his room.

****

"Gloria! Over here!"

Gloria turned to see Lynda waving and jumping up and down by the entrance to the church. John stood by her with the newspaper in his hand. The Squires, a group of boys which were an offshoot of the Knights of Columbus, the men's club, sold the newspapers as a fundraiser.

"Hi guys!" Gloria hugged her sister and brother-in-law.

"Where are the boys?" Lynda asked.

"They went ahead with your kids, I think. Maybe we'd better go get in line for our plates."

Gloria followed Lynda and John into the Parish Hall a few yards away. Tables were set up cafeteria style and covered in white tablecloths. Salt and pepper shakers and napkin holders were at each table. The smell of mesquite barbecued chicken filled the hall as well as the voices of the parish members with their children. Shrieks of laughter and running feet resounded through the place.

"Maybe we should just get the plates to go." John suggested and shoved his hands in his pants pockets.

Gloria saw her sons along with her sister's at a table by the front of the building. "Look, the kids found a table."

John harrumphed. "I guess they want to eat here."

"What are they talking about?" Lynda said, always curious about what her kids were up to.

"Who knows with kids? But Gordy may be talking about a new girl he met."

"Really?" Lynda looked at Gordy and smiled. "Aw, my baby. I hope this one's nice to him."

"I hope so, too." Gloria looked over at her youngest son and saw Dex sitting quietly. "And Dex is thinking about an SUV he might be able to buy."

"Oh good." Lynda said as the line inched up a little nearer to the food.

"Eddie told him about it."

"Eddie?" Lynda wrinkled her nose. Her sister had never liked Eddie, which had caused problems, too. "When did he come into the picture?"

"You know how he is. Disappears for months, then all of a sudden he's here and filling Dex's head with bad ideas."

Lynda put her arm around her. "I'll pray he disappears again really quickly."

Gloria laughed, but looked worriedly at Dex. "I've asked Dex to drive this SUV to the house so I can see it and talk to Eddie. He got angry with me. Told me I never let him make his own decisions. I try, but Eddie is such a charmer. He could convince birds to sing mariachi music."

Lynda smiled, "Well, yeah. He convinced you to elope with him, didn't he? Miss Smarty Pants, didn't want to get married until she was an old lady."

She tapped her sister's shoulder gently and greeted the perky lady who served her the chicken. "Hello. Busy as usual, huh, Minnie?"

"Always. Why do I keep volunteering? One of these days I'm going to quit." Minnie plopped a chicken breast on Gloria's plate and pushed her chef's hat back.

"That'll be the day, Minnie darling." A stocky older man, who was her husband, poked her in her ribs. "You wouldn't know what to do with yourself if you were always home."

"Hah! That's what you think, you old buzzard." Minnie told him and her husband walked away. "I hate to say this, but the old goat is right." Minnie whispered.

As the next lady spooned beans and potato salad onto her plate, Gloria laughed, then asked her sister, "Have you heard from Dad? Is he enjoying the cruise?"

"Yes, he called a couple of days ago. I meant to tell you." Lynda shrugged. "You know how he is. Said it was fine, but he didn't like the food, prefers his beans and rice. And told me he should have just stayed home."

"Wonder what he would think of Matt. He never liked Eddie." Gloria put a slice of bread on her plate.

"You know why," Lynda grinned. "He stole you."

Gloria laughed. "Right. He didn't ask for my hand in marriage the old-fashioned way, so he stole me."

Lynda pointed her finger at Gloria, "So inform Matt of the proper protocol that this family follows when it comes to asking for your hand in marriage."

Gloria's heart fluttered in her breast. And not because she had forgotten her medication. Marriage to Matt? She really couldn't see that happening. Everything seemed so complicated.

At the table, the kids talked among themselves, hardly paying attention to them, Gloria noticed.

"Didn't you tell me you were going out with Matt last night?" Lynda asked.

"Yes, and we did."

"How did it go?"

"Very well. We went to an Italian restaurant on the River Walk."

"How romantic. And you walked along it, right?" Her sister sighed. "Remember, we used to do that, John?"

"Eons ago." John ate his chicken.

"You should do it again. We lucked out and there weren't very many people last night."

"Is this getting serious?"

"I think so." Gloria lowered her voice and turned to see the kids were still involved in their own conversation. "But...uh..."

"What?" Lynda toyed with her beans.

"I haven't told him about my blood pressure."

"Is that a big deal? I remember at the festival you didn't want me to say anything. I meant to ask you what that was all about?"

"He seems to be afraid of illness."

"You're not ill. You're on medication. There's a difference."

"Is there?"

"Of course." Lynda stared. "You need to tell him. Your not telling him has made it an even bigger deal than it was because now you've been dishonest."

Gloria groaned. "I know."

"When are you seeing him again?"

"Later on today."

"Perfect. Tell him then. Trust is the number one most important thing in a relationship. Right, John?"

"Whatever you say, Lynda." John grinned. "Smile and nod, right Dex?"

Dex turned to his uncle and frowned.

"Smile and nod." John repeated.

"Always, *Tío*." Dex said.

Lynda poked him in the ribs with her elbow almost knocking his cup of tea down.

"Hey!" John held on to his tea.

"Behave yourself." Her sister admonished her husband. Turning to Gloria, she continued, "The other important thing is passion."

Gloria couldn't help herself. She felt her face getting red and quickly looked down to her plate.

"Ooooh." Lynda drawled out the word. "Passion exists."

Turning to the kids, Gloria scolded her sister, "Keep your voice down."

"You have to tell me everything."

"There's nothing to tell. Though I did feel a bit hypocritical in church today."

"It's about time, Sis. I'm so happy for you." Lynda had the grace to talk quietly.

John didn't say anything for which Gloria was grateful.

"But you do have to talk to him. Be honest. You'll be surprised how easy it is."

As she and the boys went back home, she hoped it would be so. She also braced herself for confronting Eddie.

Chapter Thirteen

Once home, Gloria decided to exercise. She changed into her workout clothes, navy blue sweats and tennis shoes and walked out to the shed. Breathing in the smell of the roses, she threw her arms out wide as if to hug the world. The treadmill hummed as she flipped the switch. She adjusted the incline and the rate. Placing the ear phones in her ears, she turned on her CD player. The boys kidded her, saying that she should get an MP3 player. Someday. Right now, she enjoyed listening to her seventies disco music on her old-timey CD player.

Slowly, she started walking. Lynda was right. She had to talk to Matt. He was also holding something back from her and she had to know what it was. She had to accept the fact that she had high blood pressure, but with medication, exercise and eating the right foods, she could control it. She even looked forward to a time where she wouldn't have to take pills. She also had to accept the fact that having hypertension didn't mean that she was old. It just meant that she hadn't been taking care of herself properly. Besides, heart disease ran in her family. Of course, they also ate greasy, fried foods and drank alcohol.

As Gloria walked on the treadmill, she looked down at herself. She gave a little jog. Matt made love to her last night. She had been with a man after all this time. And it had been more than she expected. Her inner thighs felt deliciously achy. Jogging a little again, she listened to a love song on her CD player and relived last night.

"Mom, phone. It's Tanya." Gordy handed her the phone and ran back inside the house.

"What's up, Tanya?"

"That man is running me ragged. What do you think he wants to do now?" Tanya's disgruntled voice came over the line.

Before Gloria could answer, Tanya continued, "He wants to expand his landscaping business to Austin. Why does he want to go over there? I hate Austin! They only have one highway and it's always crowded. I don't know anyone over there. I think I'm going to divorce him."

"Tanya, you're not serious?" Gloria turned the CD player off.

"Of course, I'm not. But what the hell does he want to do in Austin? He doesn't need any more money. He has enough. Besides, we're going on a European cruise. You know this is fate's wicked sense of humor, getting in the way of my dream again. I've always wanted to go to Europe. Why can't I go?"

"Tanya, you're whining." Gloria breathed in and out slowly. Her calves were burning and her heart rate was up a little.

"I know. I know. Oh, I'm so mad at him. I called Matt to help me talk some sense into him and I couldn't reach him. Any idea where he is? By the way, how's it going with you two? Still growing roses?"

"We're fine. Absolutely fabulous."

"Do I hear an ecstatic note in your voice? Did ya'll do it? You did, didn't you? That's the only time a woman feels ecstatic. That, and the thought of going to Europe. Wayne, where are you going? Wayne? Shit. Hold on, Gloria."

Gloria heard muffled voices, then a slammed door.

"Sorry about that, my friend. He's going for a walk. A walk? When has that man gone for a walk? He just wants to get away from me. Coward! So, what's going on with you and Matt? Better than what's going on between Wayne and me. Give me something to be happy about."

"Well, we did have a great time last night downtown at the River Walk and then..."

"You know it's been years since that man took me anywhere. I've given him the best years of my life and two children and what has he given me? Nothing, but grief. He spends more time with plants than with me. He ought to go sleep in the damn yard if he loves it so much. You know, that's what I'm going to do. I'm going to set up a bed for him out in the middle of the yard and put all his rotten junk out there, too, with him."

"Tanya, listen to me." Gloria interrupted.

"And then, I'm going to tell him that his stupid mowing equipment, edgers, and all that dirty oily machinery he keeps in the garage have to go. I want to turn it into a sewing room for myself. Yes, that's what I'm going to tell him and he can just go to Austin and stay there for all I care..." Her friend stopped on a loud sob.

"Tanya, calm yourself. How long have you and Wayne been married?"

"Twenty years," Tanya sniffled.

"Twenty years. And in all that time, has he ever not listened to you?"

"No."

"Well, then, give him a chance. You probably went off on him without giving him a chance to explain. Did he actually tell you he doesn't want to go to Europe?"

"No, but if he starts this Austin thing now, by the time the cruise comes around, he'll be knee-deep in it and won't want to leave."

"Did he say that?"

"Well, no. You're right. I didn't give him a chance to talk. I just ranted."

"When he comes back from his walk, let him talk."

"I'm sorry, Gloria." Tanya blew her nose. "Don't tell Matt anything. I'll talk to Wayne first. I do want to find out about you and Matt, but all I do is talk about me."

"What are friends for?" Gloria turned off the treadmill and walked to the bicycle. She stretched her muscles a bit before she got on. "I just have to tell him about my health issues."

"What are they? I don't think you told me the other day."

"I've got high blood pressure," Gloria admitted.

"Oh, is that it? Just take your medication and stay away from everything that tastes good. And exercise. You know what they say. Making love is good exercise. Jumping up and down in bed, raising your legs and all that. Good for every muscle of your body."

Gloria stopped pedaling the bicycle and laughed until her eyes watered. "Tanya, you're so good for me." She managed to get the words out between laughs.

Her friend's laughter echoed in her ear. "You're good for me, too. I'll let you go. The walker is back. See you later, girlfriend."

"Remember to listen."

"Okay. Okay."

Gloria hung up the phone and placed it in the basket in front of the bicycle. Just as she was about to turn on her CD player again, the phone rang. She looked at the Caller ID. Matt. Her heart jumped into her throat. She looked down at herself. She was a mess, in sweats and all sweaty.

"Hello."

"Hey. What are you up to?"

"I'm just lying about doing nothing, getting fed grapes by my boy-toy." Gloria teased.

"What?"

She laughed. "Sorry about that. I'm exercising. Can't you tell from my hard breathing?"

"Hard breathing? That reminds me of something else." Matt's deep voice caused her heart to flutter again.

"Ah yes. Me, too."

"So, how was the barbecue?"

"Very tasty, but very filling. That's why I'm exercising." Gloria looked in the direction of the landscape picture in front of her, but seeing Matt instead. "I was also sleepy, but memories of last night had me unable to relax to take a nap."

Matt's laugh rumbled in her ear. "I've been working all day. I need more workers and no one wants to stick around, claim it's too hot, it's too hard. But, I'm about done. Do you still want me to come over?"

"Oh yes." Gloria stopped pedaling. Her breathing was coming far too fast and it wasn't all due to the exertion of exercise, but to Matt. He was coming. "My sons will be here, though. They might suddenly come up with plans that can't be broken."

"Then, I'll have you all to myself."

"The idea does appeal."

"I'll be there tonight."

When she hung up, Gloria looked at herself again. Quickly, she pedaled the bicycle for ten more minutes, then decided that was enough.

Inside the house, the coolness of the AC made her shiver because she was so sweaty.

"Boys, where are you?"

Gordy ambled in from his room. "Dex is outside with

Dad. They brought the SUV over."

"Your dad is here?" She looked at herself, in workout clothes and sweating. Well, she wasn't trying to impress Eddie.

"Mom, Dex asked me to tell you not to get mad. Please, he said."

Gloria's heart melted and tears pricked her eyes. Her poor baby, always caught in the middle with her and her ex. "I'll try, Gordy, but your dad riles me up."

She opened the front door and saw a sparkling maroon SUV. Was it new? Immediately, she knew that Dex couldn't afford it. The heat of the sun blasted her after the coolness inside. Both Eddie and Dex stood admiring the vehicle.

"Hey, Mom! Look at this. It's the kind of truck I've always wanted" Dex exclaimed as soon as he saw her. He ran around to open the passenger door for her. "Get in. Look at the inside. It's clean."

Clean. Gloria knew that meant more than not dirty. It meant he liked it. She climbed inside the truck.

"It's beautiful, son, but your mom is the real beauty here." Eddie grinned and peeked in at Gloria. The whiff of his cologne filled her nostrils. Today, the only memory the smell evoked was of past arguments, which continued to this day.

"Stop it, Eddie. I'm sweaty and far from a beauty. Don't try your charm on me. It doesn't work anymore." She scolded him. Staring at him, dressed in jeans and navy blue T-shirt, she admitted he was a nice-looking man. Always had been. But, she'd never been able to trust him.

"What do you think, Mom?" Dex asked.

"It's really nice, Dex. You know I want you to have what you want. But, you know you have to be practical. You're still in school and only have a part-time job."

"I know, Mom. But I've been able to save up." Her son's eyes shone with excitement. She hated to throw cold water on his dream. "How much is it? Did you get it from a dealer?"

"The cost doesn't matter when it's a boy's first real truck." Eddie interjected.

"Of course, it matters. What kind of a thing is that to

say? Eddie, where is your brain? Dex doesn't make the kind of money to afford this type of vehicle." Gloria looked at Dex with an apology in her eyes for doing the exact thing he had requested she not do—argue with his dad, but Eddie was such an idiot.

"Mom, I've figured it out—" Dex began.

"I'll help him out," Eddie said, his eyes twinkling.

Gloria stepped out of the SUV. "Stay in the truck, Dex." The next door neighbor waved. Always working on his yard that man. Why couldn't he have stayed inside today? She waved back and pushed Eddie toward the driveway so the neighbor or Dex couldn't hear them.

"Eddie, you won't help him and you know it. You'll let him down again and then he'll be stuck with a vehicle he can't afford. Why do you do this to him? Time and time again. Damn you! I hate you sometimes." She glared at her ex, then turned to look at Dex, still in the SUV, looking down at the steering wheel.

Tears pricked her eyes again. She smacked Eddie on his chest.

"Ow!" Eddie stepped back. "You always were so passionate around me."

"Stop it. I'm angry with you. Go over there and tell Dex you were wrong. Apologize to him for crushing his dreams again. If you really want to help, find an SUV he can afford, one that won't have him in debt for five years." She flicked his forehead with her finger. "Use your brain. I know you have one."

Dex stood in front of the truck and looked at her with sad eyes. "Mom, I won't buy it. I knew I couldn't afford it as soon as I saw it. You're right. Dad, let's take it back, so I can get my old black truck."

Eddie looked as if he might dissuade his son, but only said, "Okay, son."

Dex strolled around the brilliant maroon-colored SUV and climbed in.

"You do like to make him unhappy, don't you?" Eddie taunted.

Gloria wished she had something to throw at him. "You do that, Eddie. You never think of consequences. Just want to make yourself a big man in your sons' eyes. Don't you know that all you need to do is be there for them, making things easier, not harder."

"Like you do, huh?"

"Yes."

"What do you think your dating this stranger is doing to them?"

"I should think they'd be used to seeing strangers with their parents as their dad always has a new woman in his life."

"You're not me and you know it. And they know it."

"Get out of here, Eddie. Please don't come back."

Gloria waved to Dex, blew him a kiss and marched away. He hung his head. Gordy came out of the house.

"Gordy, come with us." Eddie invited.

"No thanks, Dad. I'm washing my clothes."

Eddie looked down, then smiled. "Okay."

Gloria stared after her ex. She knew Gordy didn't lie to his dad, so he must have thrown in a load of clothes in the washer. However, Eddie probably wondered why his youngest son would prefer to do laundry instead of being with his dad. Maybe he did care how Gordy reacted to him. But, it was his own fault. He had never made the effort.

****

When Dex returned, he went straight to the kitchen. "I'm hungry. What's there to eat?" He opened the refrigerator.

"I think there's stuff for sandwiches." Gloria answered from the armchair in the living room. She had showered and changed into jeans. Matt would be here soon.

"Dex, are you all right?" She looked toward the dining table where he sat with bread, luncheon meat and other sandwich fixings.

"I don't want sandwiches." Gordy entered the kitchen and to the table and pushed his brother.

"Matt is coming over in about an hour or two." Gloria put her arms around herself. "It's cold in here." She went to check the thermostat, then stood near the dining table. "Dex?"

"I'm fine. I don't want to talk about it."

"Why is Matt coming tonight?" Gordy demanded.

"On a Sunday?" Dex began to make his sandwich.

"Why not? And what if it is Sunday?"

"You always say that you don't like to do anything on a Sunday so we can get ready for work and school on Monday." Gordy reminded her.

"Yes, I do say that, don't I?" Gloria returned to the armchair and looked at her boys, both now at the dining table. "I want to see Matt. He won't be here very long. He's been working all day, too. But, we had a really good time last night and we want to see each other again."

"Let's go eat somewhere, Dex." Gordy turned to leave.

"Yeah, that's a good idea." Her older son began to put everything back in the refrigerator.

"Boys, this is important to me. I know I haven't had a man in my life for as long as you can remember. But...well...I met Matt and he...well, I think he can become a very important part of my life. Do you understand?"

"Do you mean he's going to come live with us?" Dex's eyes were huge. "I'm moving out."

"We haven't talked about that. Right now, we just enjoy each other's company and you kids, his kids, are part of our lives and we can't ignore you, but we can't ignore each other either."

"I don't like this." Dex went to the key holder on the wall by the door and grabbed his keys. "Come on, Gordy."

"Boys." Gloria stood.

"We'll be back, Mom." Dex said. "Man, what a day!"

"You said it." Gordy closed the door.

****

The doorbell rang. Gloria looked around the living room. She had cleared off the coffee table and had stashed the boys' clothes that they were prone to leave hanging on the armchairs in their room. The kitchen table featured a centerpiece of flowers and unscented candles, which she had lit. She rushed to the door.

"Hi, Matt," Gloria greeted.

"Hi yourself." Matt leaned toward her and kissed her. "You smell so nice. A lot better than dirt and mowed grass."

"Poor baby." Gloria put her arms around him and stayed near. She put her head on his chest since she couldn't reach his shoulder.

135

"I'm almost finished at the yard I worked in today. This poor lady's yard was in a mess. Overgrown with weeds, almost reached up to my shoulders in some places. Her bushes and shrubs needed trimming. I'm not complaining. It means work for me and money, but today, there was only one place I wanted to be."

"I missed you, too. Thought about you all day. Even in church." Gloria lifted her head and Matt kissed her again. His warm lips did a sweet assault on hers. She forgot about Eddie, the SUV and even her son's sadness.

"I didn't even ask. Are your sons here? I noticed Dex's truck isn't here."

"They went to eat. Dex is a bit upset."

"About my coming over?"

"Well, yes. Both him and Gordy. I had a talk with them. Come sit down."

"What did you say?" Matt dropped into the sofa.

Gloria curled up beside Matt. "I told them that you were becoming an important part of my life."

"I feel the same way." He kissed her again.

She was swept away on a wave of feeling, then murmured. "Do you want something to drink?"

"No, don't move."

Her heart skipped a bit and shivers ran up and down her body as Matt's lips captured her own again. Before she knew what he was about, he was on top of her on the sofa. She brought her legs around him, but then she heard a car door.

"My sons are back. I thought they were going to be gone for awhile." Gloria pushed Matt away and waited for her sons to walk in. She smoothed her hair down.

"I don't think it was them," Matt shrugged. "But I guess this isn't the right time or place."

"Let me get us something to drink. Okay?"

"Fine." Matt grabbed the T.V. remote and flipped channels.

"Look at my roses. Aren't they pretty?" Gloria pointed to a vase of roses on the mantel.

In the kitchen, Gloria breathed in and out. She wanted Matt, but her sons could come in at any minute. Of course, they could go to her room. But, she couldn't do that, either. She always told her sons that one of the rules of the house was that she didn't want them bringing girls over to have sex. As they got older, she realized that the rule had to apply to her, too.

"Lemon-lime soda, okay? That's all I have." Gloria handed the glass to Matt.

"I'll take it." Matt took the soda and pulled her down next to him.

"So, what else was Dex upset about?"

"His dad almost convinced him to buy a practically brand new SUV. He was here earlier trying to convince me that it was a good idea."

"Your ex-husband was here? I thought he never came around. I mean you never mention him." Matt drank, but kept his eyes on her.

"That's because we've been divorced for a long time and because he disappears for months. When he does show up, he usually disrupts everything."

"I'm sorry."

"It's not your fault. But he built up this idea of the truck for Dex and now he feels bad about the whole thing. I do, too. It's a big mess."

"Maybe I can help. I've got a friend who's a mechanic. He buys old cars, works on them, then sells them for a profit. What do you think?"

Gloria's heart lifted and she hugged Matt. "Really? That sounds good. But how old are these cars? Dex doesn't want a jalopy."

Matt grinned. "Believe me, rose princess, I was a young dude once and I know how important the right wheels are."

"Yes, look into that for Dex, please. It'll make him feel so much better." She was practically in love with Matt already and anyone who was nice to her sons always deserved a gold star in her book. She kept her arm around him and grinned.

"What about you? You know, I have an ulterior motive for helping, don't you?"

"Do you? Well, I'm all yours."

He set his drink on the coffee table, leaned towards her, and captured her lips. As usual, her senses engulfed her and she could only feel.

The dryer's timer went off. Gordy had forgotten about

his laundry.

Matt lifted his head. "What was that?"

"The dryer. Let me go get the clothes out or they'll wrinkle. And I'll refill your drink. I won't be long."

When Gloria returned, she felt dizzy. Matt wavered before her eyes. "Oh. I feel light-headed." She put her head between her knees and breathed slowly in and out.

"Are you all right?" Matt asked from far away it seemed.

"Yes, I'm just feeling a little dizzy—and hot." She sat up and waved her hand in front of her face.

"I wouldn't mind that," he said, his face screwed up with concern, "but you don't look well."

"Maybe my BP went up." At his puzzled expression, she explained, "Blood pressure. I should have told you a long time ago, but you always seemed to close up whenever illness was mentioned. But, I want to be honest with you if we're going to have a relationship."

"You have high blood pressure? You kept something like that from me?" Matt stood up.

"I'm sorry, but it makes me feel really old."

Matt wasn't looking at her anymore. He was staring at the roses, on which he hadn't commented before. And his shoulders slumped and then he hung his head. "You lied to me."

"I didn't lie. I kept the truth from you. How many times do you want me to apologize? I know I should have told you, but..."

"Are you sure you're okay?"

"Yes. The dizziness has passed. It comes and goes. The doctor adjusts my medication. We haven't found the right dosage so I won't have such side effects."

"Good. Listen, your roses should be fine for awhile. I'll tell Wayne what I did. He should be able to take care of any further problems you may have."

"Matt..." Gloria began.

He turned away and walked toward the door.

"What's the matter, Matt? Are you leaving already?" Gloria followed him, tears filling her eyes. Her heart lodged in her heart. "Tell me what's going on."

"You're sick. I can't deal with that."

"What?" Gloria sat on the arm of the sofa chair, her

legs suddenly feeling weak, but not from dizziness. Just because she had high blood pressure, Matt was leaving her? What kind of man was he? No wonder his ex-wife had wanted to kill him. She could kill him now.

But—she loved him. For once in her life, she had met a man who she could see fitting in with her sons and her sister. He could be a part of her family. Everything wasn't perfect, but it was nothing they couldn't work through. She knew her sons loved her. If she just reassured them that her love for them wouldn't change and that Matt would never replace their dad, they would eventually accept Matt. She was sure of it. As she was sure, Matt's daughters would come to accept her. However, he didn't want to deal with a sick woman. The tears wouldn't stop. Her heart beat rapidly and for a second she was breathless. She watched as Matt turned the knob on the door.

"I'm sorry, Gloria." He looked at her. She knew he could see her tears. But he didn't comment.

"Me, too, Matt. I made a mistake. I always do that with men. Well, in other things, too, but mostly with men. You haven't told me why. I mean, everybody gets sick. I'm sure your daughters get sick. You get sick. We're human." Gloria brushed the tears away with a fast sweep of her hand. She didn't want to cry.

"My mom had high blood pressure." He looked at the door, not at her.

In spite of herself, Gloria's interest was piqued.

"She started with high blood pressure, ended up having bypass surgery. Her veins were all messed up. Through the years, she had never taken care of her health. High cholesterol. Fatty diet. Everything they caution about now. She died." Matt turned to her, his brown eyes begging her to understand. "I can't go through that again."

"I'm not going to die, Matt. At least, not any time soon."

"But there's the risk."

"You could die on the way home tonight. What makes you such an authority on dying anyway? Do you have some inside line?"

"I'm sorry, Gloria. I can't do this. I wish I could, but I

can't." His voice sounded hoarse.

Gloria watched him leave and almost ran after him to have him explain further. But after the fiasco earlier with Eddie and the SUV and now this, she couldn't do it. Instead she thought it better he left. Good riddance! She didn't need any man in her life, and around her sons, especially a weakling. Hadn't she learned that already? If he wanted a perfectly healthy woman, she was sure he could find one. More power to him!

In spite of everything, the tears wouldn't stop falling, spilling down her cheeks. She feared she would start sobbing. Where were her sons? She had to pull herself together before they got home. Gloria ran to her room and threw herself on her bed. However much she told herself she was well rid of Matt, she couldn't convince her heart—that blasted organ which wouldn't work properly, physically or emotionally.

Chapter Fourteen

Last night when her sons had returned, she had been in bed, had been unable to get out of it. She knew her eyes were red with all the crying she had done. Not wanting them to see her in such sad shape, she had pretended to be asleep and mumbled a good night to them. This morning, though, she had to crawl out of bed.

"See you tonight, boys." Gloria cleared her throat.

Both of them just moved in their beds. Well, summer was almost over and school would start. They deserved a break. Gordy didn't go in to work until noon.

She slid the patio door open and looked at her roses. They looked so much better. Walking toward the patio table, she wished she could say the same about herself. Matt had revived her roses, but had destroyed her. Tears filled her eyes again. Well, she didn't need him in her life. She had lived all these years without a man and she could continue to do so. Her chest felt as if she had been punched. Maybe it wouldn't hurt so much if they hadn't made love. He had not only taken her body, but her heart. She had given herself completely to him. Oh! It made her so angry. She saw a rake leaning against the house. She picked it up and whacked one of her rose bushes. A few rose petals fluttered to the ground. She whacked it again. Then, she leaned over the rake and let the tears fall. "Weakling! I don't need him. I'm glad he's gone."

Gloria threw the rake to the ground, looked at her dilapidated rose bush and ran inside the house. Splashing water on her face, she washed any trace of tears. Hurriedly, she put more makeup on and left for work.

At the office, Beatrice found her eating a cinnamon roll and drinking tea.

"I thought you couldn't eat that." Her friend commented.

"I can't, but it was a hell of a weekend." Gloria tore a piece of roll and popped it into her mouth.

"You look as if you've been crying."

Gloria felt the tears coming again. "That's because I have been."

"What happened?"

"Oh, he left me. Just like all men do. Things get too hard and too complicated and they can't deal with it. Men! I hate them all."

"They can be a handful. Look at what I have to deal with at home." Beatrice creased her face in concern. "But, I thought you and Matt were working on a more long-term relationship."

"Apparently not."

"Tell me."

"I told him about my high blood pressure."

"And that made him leave you?" Beatrice frowned.

"Doesn't make sense, does it? He did tell me that his mom had died of it, well, of complications. She had bypass surgery. He did say it was due to a life of not taking care of herself. He says he can't deal with that again."

"You're not that bad. It's just high blood pressure. I mean, not just, it's not something you fool around with, but really, what is his problem?"

"I don't know, but he left me. And we had such a good time on Saturday night. We went downtown to the river, had dinner, kissed—and all." Gloria smiled in spite of herself.

Her friend grinned and saluted her with her cup of coffee. "Really? Wow, it's about time."

"And now what? He left me. If I didn't know better, I'd say he just wanted to get into my pants."

"Well, maybe..." Beatrice leered.

"Oh, you. I don't think that was it. He seemed to really care about me."

"You need to call him and talk to him some more. Maybe he just hasn't faced all the feelings that surfaced around his mom's death. Maybe he's suppressed them."

"Now, you're a psychologist, huh?"

"No, but I know men. They don't express their feelings and when they do they come out all wrong. They're hurt, they get angry. They're tired, they get angry. They're hungry, they get angry. See what I mean?"

Carolyn's voice came over the paging system. "Gloria,

line one."

"There he is. He couldn't wait another minute without talking to you." Beatrice left for her office.

Gloria hurried to her office and picked up the phone. "Yes, this is Gloria."

"Mrs. Amaya, I'm Celeste Hinojosa. I run an independent bookstore called Books for All and I have your resume here."

"Yes, I remember." Gloria stopped herself from divulging that she had sent a resume to every bookstore in town.

"I notice that you don't have experience in retail, however, your cover letter really impressed me."

"Thank you."

A ruffle of papers greeted her statement. "I'd like to schedule an appointment for an interview, say today, or tomorrow. I'm really anxious to fill this position."

"Are you open at noon? That's when I take my lunch hour. I could go today. I don't think you're too far away from me."

"No, I'm not. And yes, noon would be just fine. I'll see you then, Mrs. Amaya. I'm looking forward to meeting you."

Gloria hung up the phone and didn't know what to feel. Her eyes burned with all the tears she had shed over Matt. However, she had an interview at a bookstore. It wasn't a job offer, but the woman had been impressed with her cover letter. What had she written on that thing? For the life of her, she couldn't remember a single word.

"Was it Matt?" Beatrice called from her office.

"No." Gloria walked across the hall and stood in the door way of her friend's office.

"Remember, when we talked about looking for another job? I sent out resumes to bookstores. You know I've always wanted to do that. Someone just called me from Books for All and wants to interview me."

"Oh no. I don't want you to leave," Beatrice wailed.

"It's not a sure thing. Don't worry yet."

"They'll hire you. Why wouldn't they? You're a good worker and you love books. What more could they want?"

"I don't have any retail experience. I do have a degree in business, though, and I have done billing and collections in the medical field anyway."

"When are you going?"

"At lunch."

"I know you're going to leave."

"Maybe it won't be enough money. It is an independent bookstore after all. The chains get all the business."

Gloria could tell her friend wasn't convinced by the way she kept typing furiously on her keyboard.

"Good morning." Liz stood behind Gloria laden with binders and a big black bag.

"Good morning. What do you have there?" Gloria took some of the binders from her hands.

"I've read these all weekend long trying to understand this thing that Kedco is doing. And you know what? It's voluntary participation. We don't have to join if we don't want to. And I don't want to. I know we're going to have to do this at some point and they are changing the way we'll get paid, but not for another two years. In those two years, we'll get ready. We'll set up all the protocols and policies necessary."

"Are you sure, Liz? Sometimes, it's not wise to put off doing something." Gloria almost bit her tongue at that. If she had told Matt about her high blood pressure, he never would have stayed around long enough to take her mind, body and soul.

"I found out about another thing. There's an initiative we can join. We'll do everything as if the new payment system has been implemented, but we won't actually start getting paid that way until after two years." Liz nodded. "Isn't that good?"

"Are we going to have new forms?" Beatrice asked from inside her office.

Gloria moved from the doorway so Liz could enter Beatrice's office. "No, the forms will stay the same at the beginning. It'll be a slow process. But it won't be as sudden as this other one. And actually, I think they're going to do away with it. I don't know of any agency that's ready to jump into the new payment system." Liz walked toward her office. "When the field staff come in for the morning report, I'm going to call the office staff in and I'll tell everyone. My worries are over—at least for two years."

"At least when you tell her you're leaving, she won't wring her hands, or your neck since the crisis is over." Beatrice threw a stack of timesheets in her "out" tray.

"You're so good for me, friend." Gloria returned to her office. Sighing, she threw herself into her work and refused to think about Matt.

****

Books For All, situated in a shopping strip center off of Loop 410, near Crossroads Mall, was almost hidden between a nail shop and a tax office. Gloria liked the fact that it was only a few minutes away from Home Nursing. The amount of time she spent on her commute wouldn't change that much.

Gloria parked and walked toward the bookstore. The glass door jingled as she opened it. The smell of print filled the air. She inhaled deeply. The smell of new books—her favorite smell. Next, to Matt's spicy cologne, came the unbidden thought. Gloria pushed that thought firmly from her mind.

Shelves of books lined the walls and covered the center of the store. Signs indicating fiction, mystery and art had been posted above corresponding shelves. Pictures and posters of the classics, children's authors and bestsellers were pinned above the shelves on the walls. The checkout counter was near the door and this is where Gloria waited.

"Hello! Who's there?" A high-pitched voice called out from behind the counter.

"Gloria Amaya. I'm here for an interview." Gloria leaned over the counter.

"Oh yes. Come on back. Jenny just stepped out for lunch."

Following the voice, Gloria made her way around the counter and entered a hallway. At the end, stood Celeste Hinojosa, a petite woman dressed in beige Capri pants and light green no-sleeves blouse. Her blond hair was curly and seemed almost too big for her head. She waved Gloria over.

"Come in, Mrs. Amaya. Sit down."

"Please call me Gloria." She looked around at the office. The desk was piled high with papers and books.

The walls were covered with more posters of authors.

"You can see I need help." Celeste opened a manila folder on her lap. "Gloria. I have a sister by that name. As I told you, I was very impressed with your cover letter. You have a love of books that came through loud and clear. You even like the way they smell."

"Oh yes, especially new books. That's what this store smells like."

"Yes, it does, doesn't it? I've tried different air fresheners, lemon, pine, rose." The woman wrinkled her nose. "But, you know, I don't like rose scent. It can't be duplicated. Only the real thing will do for me."

Roses, yes. That's what had gotten her into trouble. Printer's ink—that's the scent she would concentrate on now. But now, she agreed with Celeste.

"You have a degree. That shows that you stick to a goal. Plus, you've been at your job for ten years. Nowadays, that says a lot, too. Jenny has only been with me for two months. I'm keeping my fingers crossed that she'll stay. But, you never know."

Gloria waited as Celeste continued to examine her resume and cover letter.

"How much do you get paid now?" Her prospective employer picked up a pen from the clutter on her desk.

Gloria told her.

"Wow. Really?" Celeste continued writing in the folder and her forehead wrinkled in concentration.

Gloria fiddled with the strap of her purse. "I feared I would run into that problem. The medical and home health fields have been my areas of expertise for a long time. However, as you said I do have a business degree and I am familiar with billing and collections. I also worked as a bookkeeper for a time."

"Yes, I see." The woman closed the folder. "I like you, Gloria. I think you would fit in here really well. Let me crunch some numbers and see what I can come up with. I'll call you by the end of the week. When could you start?"

"I'd have to give at least two weeks' notice, maybe a little bit longer since I have been with the company so long and my replacement will be brand new."

"I see." Celeste looked at the folder again.

Probably looking at her salary. Gloria wondered if

she should have said a lower number, but she really couldn't get less than she was making in order to provide for herself and her boys. At least Celeste had called her in. She hadn't been on an interview in years. She'd mark this down to experience.

Celeste stood. "Thanks for coming in, Gloria."

"Thank you. And now that I know you're here I'll come by during my lunch hour. I didn't know this bookstore was here before. I'm always looking for a quiet place to read."

The woman smiled. "Come in anytime. We're open until five most days, only on Wednesdays until nine."

Gloria left and drove back to work. The afternoon was long. She couldn't concentrate. First, thoughts of Matt invaded her brain, then thoughts of the interview. In spite of knowing that Celeste wouldn't call her, she still hoped she would. In spite of telling herself that she never wanted to hear from Matt again, she found herself looking at her phone every time she heard Carolyn answer and hoped that her phone would start ringing because the receptionist had transferred a call. She received many calls, but none from Matt. Her head began to hurt as well as her eyes.

****

Carolyn's voice sounded over the intercom. "Gloria, line three."

Matt! No, she didn't want it to be Matt. That was over and done with and she was much the better for it. She refused to acknowledge the throbbing pain at her temples.

"This is Gloria. May I help you?"

"Gloria, this is Celeste Hinojosa. We spoke at lunch."

She sat up straighter in her chair. "Of course."

"I've interviewed three other people this afternoon."

Gloria sighed. "Yes." Celeste was making a courtesy call. The standard: *Thank you for applying, but we found someone more qualified.* Her heart sank and the pain in her head and her eyes zinged her with force. She opened the desk drawer to her right and fished the bottle of aspirin out. Quickly, she took two with the glass of water she had on her desk.

"I want to make you an offer." Celeste said.

Not hearing what Celeste said next, Gloria said, "Well, thank you for at least giving me an inter—I'm sorry, what?"

"I want to offer you the job. I can match your salary. I want someone who will really devote herself to the bookstore and not just come in here on a trial basis. You strike me as someone who wants this job, not necessarily just because of the money."

"Yes, I do." Gloria sat up straighter and wondered at the potency of the aspirin. Her pains were not so severe now. Her heart beat faster and she wanted to stand up and shout. She had done it. She was going to work at a bookstore.

"Good. You told me you needed to give two or three weeks' notice, right? What if you start at the first of the month? That'll give you four weeks. I've gone without an assistant for awhile now, I can wait a little longer."

"Thank you so much, Celeste."

"You're welcome. We'll see you soon."

Gloria hung up and twirled around in her chair. "Yay!"

When she turned to face the door, Beatrice stood there. "What's going on?"

"I'm going to work at a bookstore. I got the job."

"That was quick. You just went on the interview at noon."

"I know. I really didn't think she'd call me. But she did." Gloria stomped her feet in quick succession at her chair. "She did." And she whirled around again.

She looked at her friend's downcast expression. "I'm sorry, Beatrice. I know you don't think this is good news. I've wanted this for a long time. I can't wait to start. And I'm not that far away. It's on Fred Road. That's just down the street."

"It won't be the same."

"We can have lunch sometimes."

Her friend smiled faintly. "Maybe at first. But then you'll get busy and we'll drift apart."

"No, we won't." Gloria assured her friend. "We've known each other for ten years. Do you think I would just walk off and not keep in touch?"

"When are you going to tell Liz?"

"Oh, that's right." She stood up. "No time like the present. As you said this morning, with the crisis over, maybe she won't panic too much."

Beatrice hugged her. "I'll miss you."

Gloria pat her friend on the back. "As much as I'll miss seeing your face. Better go brave the old girl."

Her comment made her friend laugh. Gloria walked down the hall to Liz's office and found her hidden behind a stack of binders.

"What are you doing, Liz?"

"Trying to get organized." She peeked above the binders. "I don't think it's working. What's up?"

"I have to talk to you. May I close the door?" Gloria did.

"Uh oh. This sounds serious."

"I have to give you my notice. I've found another job."

Liz looked at the floor where more binders were stacked. "I knew you would. With another home health agency?"

"No, actually, at a bookstore." Gloria grinned.

"At a bookstore? What are you going to do there? You won't make enough money to support your family, will you?"

"As a matter of fact, yes. She offered me the same amount as I make here. Can you believe it? I can't, since it's an independent bookstore, not a chain. I'm sure even a chain wouldn't pay me what I make here. At least, not at an entry level job."

"Why is she paying you? Do you trust her?" Liz wrinkled her nose.

"Why shouldn't I? She liked my attitude and my cover letter." Gloria told her boss who remained silent. "I'll be sorry to leave. I've enjoyed my time here at Home Nursing. I've learned a lot, thanks to you."

"I'll miss you, too. You do realize you have to give me time to replace you, right? I want you to train this new person, too. Three weeks at least." Liz pushed the stack of binders out of the way. Two of them fell to the floor.

Gloria picked them up. "Yes, of course."

"Okay. Well. I'll put an ad in the paper tomorrow. Thanks for telling me."

At Liz's dejected look, she made her way out of the

office, stopped at Beatrice's door. "I told her. Three weeks from now I'll be gone."

"Boo-hoo. I already miss you." Beatrice said. "Who's going to help me when I have computer problems?"

"You can always call me at my new job," Gloria grinned.

"Get out of my office before I throw something at you. You traitor!"

Gloria laughed and returned to her desk, looked at all the items on it, her phone, her computer, the stack-up trays and her throat closed up. Tears pricked her eyes. But, then, she whispered, "I'm going to work at a bookstore." And she whirled around in her chair again. "Yay."

Chapter Fifteen

"Boys, I got a job at a bookstore." Gloria announced as soon as she walked in the door to her house. She saw the sofa where she and Matt had almost made love and sadness enveloped her.

But then, Dex walked in the room. "What bookstore? Didn't you say you couldn't make enough money working there?"

"That's what's so wonderful about this. The lady is going to pay me what I make now. She must be wealthy. Otherwise, her doing that doesn't make sense."

Gordy jogged towards her and gave her a tight squeeze.

"*Ay*, Gordy! I'm a girl."

He laughed. "Did you tell us the name of the bookstore?"

"Oh, no I didn't. Books for All."

Both her sons burst out laughing. "What a name! Sounds like a place you would work at, Mom," Dex said.

"Have you heard from your dad?" Gloria knew her son still saw that polished SUV in his mind.

"No. I probably won't hear from him again for another long while," Dex sighed.

The phone rang. "I'll get it," Gordy said. Then, handed the cordless phone to Dex, who went to his room with it.

"I'm going to go change. See what's in the refrigerator to eat," Gloria told Gordy.

"Mom, that was Matt," Dex said at the doorway of her room.

"Matt?" Gloria couldn't speak. Her heart had lodged in her throat.

"He says he has a truck he wants me to see. He's bringing it over in a few minutes. I told him that was fine. It is, isn't it?"

Gloria pulled a white T-shirt over her head. Her

heart sang. He was coming. He was coming. But then, she sobered up. He wasn't visiting because of her.

"Mom?"

"Yes, Dex." Gloria sat on her bed.

"Are you dressed?" Her son asked.

"Yes, come in."

"Why is he bringing a truck? Did you talk to him about this?"

"Well, you seemed so sad yesterday when you had to take back that other one. I just mentioned it to Matt last night. He said he has a friend who works on old cars."

"That's what he told me." Dex's eyes moved from side to side in his face as he did when he thought hard about something, or was about to throw a fit.

"Are you angry with me?"

"Not if this truck is good. Do you think it will be?"

"Wait until you see it. Don't make any decisions now, or a quick one, either. Take your time."

Dex hugged her. "Thanks, Mom."

"Any time, *mijo*. You know I'd do anything for you."

"Anything?" He teased her.

"Within reason."

Her son left the room and she heard him talking to Gordy. She could hear the excitement in his voice. Matt was a good man. He had quirks. That's all. Too late for romance. What had she been thinking?

When Matt arrived, Dex hurried out the door. Gordy ran after him. Never had her sons run out to meet Matt like that. Of course, the SUV was the attraction. Should she go outside? She'd better. Otherwise, she'd have a lot of explaining to do. She heaved a big sigh and pulled open the front door.

"Mom, look at it. I like it," Dex said, practically running around the truck.

"Yeah, fool. It's better than that mustard-colored job you looked at." Gordy reminded his brother.

Gloria sneaked a glance at Matt, who avoided her eyes. Then, she focused her attention on the SUV, black with silver, smaller than yesterday's.

She cleared her throat. "Pretty nice."

"Get in, Mom." Dex invited from the driver's seat. Gordy was already inside turning on the stereo.

Gloria climbed in the back, slid to the center of the seat and leaned over to look at the black dashboard. The inside had gray seat covers.

"Man, listen to those speakers." Her youngest son exclaimed. "Your music will sound great in here."

Dex lowered the volume of the stereo as Matt spoke.

"It's got a new set of tires." Matt said. "And Jason practically put in a new engine. It's got a lot of miles, but it'll last you a good while if you maintain it."

"Oh, yeah, the unimportant stuff, right, Mom?" Her son grinned from ear to ear, so excited about his potential new vehicle.

She looked towards Matt again and caught him doing the same. Her heart flew to her throat and she averted her glance.

"You want to take it for a drive?" Matt asked.

"Can I?" Dex asked, his eyes shining.

Matt threw the keys at him. "Sure. Let's go."

He climbed into the back seat where Gloria sat in the middle. His cologne filled the air and the scent of his body reminded her of the closeness they had shared. Not looking at him, she moved to the end of the seat.

He asked. "Don't you want to come along?"

Her body ached to be close to him. But, she refused to pretend that everything was all right for longer than necessary. "No, you go ahead." She climbed out. "Be careful, though. Don't have an accident. You might die." Gloria taunted and this time she did look straight into his eyes.

Matt frowned.

Gordy shrugged his shoulders.

Dex raised his eyebrows. "Come on, Mom. Die? We're just going for a drive."

She watched as her older son backed out of the driveway with a big grin on his face. Matt sat in the middle of the backseat. Gordy rode in the front.

The sun wasn't so hot and the wind was blowing. It looked as if it might rain. Finally, her sons were communicating with Matt, had gone off on a drive with him and things were a mess between them. Admittedly, they wouldn't have gone if Matt hadn't brought a truck for Dex. But they were together and talking, her sons and

Matt. What could be better than that? Well, it could. She should be with them. And she and Matt shouldn't have separated. But no, she was well rid of him. If he couldn't understand a simple diagnosis of hypertension, what would he do if, God forbid, she contracted some kind of cancer later on in her life? These things occurred. She tended to think that they happened to other people, but sometimes they touched close to home.

She turned to walk back into the house, but heard a vehicle. It was Dex. He jumped out of the SUV and slammed the door. "Mom, I don't want any charity. Just because you're going out with him doesn't mean that you have to make deals for me."

"Dex, what are you talking about?"

She looked towards Matt, who stood by the passenger door. He shrugged and lifted up both hands, palms up. He didn't know what was happening either.

"This truck supposedly costs $5,000. What a coincidence. That's how much I've saved up. Man, what a set of parents. First, Dad. Now, you. Leave me alone to make my own mistakes." Her son marched to the front door.

"*Mijo*, wait a minute." Gloria held him back.

Gordy stayed by the truck, not saying a word, but his face showed that he felt the same way as his older brother.

"Dex, I didn't make a deal with your mom. And it's not charity. But, it does seem to be a coincidence about the money. Jason really did tell me he'd sell it for $5,000. If I were you, I'd talk him a bit down. You still have to pay tax, title and license." Matt explained.

"It's for real? I can buy this truck?" Dex's angry demeanor lessened.

"That's why I brought it over here to you. Jason will stand by the work he did on it. If you have any problems, just take it back to him."

"Sounds too good to be true." Dex stared at the black and silver SUV, not as new as the maroon one, but more affordable and guaranteed.

"Sometimes, something comes along that does sound too good to be true." Gloria put her arm around her son's shoulders. "And isn't it wonderful when it turns out to be just good?"

Gloria couldn't help a glance towards Matt. He was staring at her, and she looked away quickly.

"Yeah!" Dex exclaimed.

Gordy strolled up to them. "So, wuss, are you buying the truck, or are you going to stand around talking all day?"

"I'm buying," Dex decided.

"Good choice," Matt said.

She watched as her son and Matt made arrangements to meet at Jason's place and get the paperwork for the title the next day.

"So, I'll see you tomorrow, Dex. Bye." Matt climbed into the truck and waved in the general direction of all of them, not singling her out.

"Why is he leaving, Mom? Don't you want to be alone?" Gordy asked in a sing-song voice.

"He has to take the truck back." Gloria stared as Matt drove off. Her heart felt heavy and tears threatened to spill again. She blinked them away rapidly. To avoid questions, she shouted, because she had just remembered it, "Insurance. We'll have to add it to the insurance policy."

Her sons laughed, forgetting about Matt so easily she was certain. She wished she could do the same.

****

Dex and Gordy decided to go to the movies that Friday night.

"Do you want to come, Mom?" Gordy asked.

Her older son added, "Yeah, I'll take you for a drive in the new SUV." Dex had been driving around in his truck ever since he and Matt had finished with the paperwork.

Usually, she liked going to the movies with her sons. She was always amazed when they invited her. Tonight, though, she declined. "I just want to curl up in the chair and read a book or watch a movie here. I'll be fine. Ya'll go ahead. You can give me a ride later, son."

"Is Matt coming over?" Dex wanted to know.

"No, not tonight." Gloria looked at the T.V.

"Is he gone for good?" Gordy grinned hopefully.

"I don't know." Gloria adjusted the blanket around

herself. It was still summer, but she felt like cuddling under a blanket.

"Are you sick, or did you have a fight?" Dex, who had been at the door, went to sit on the sofa. "You look as if you've been crying."

"I don't want to talk about it right now, boys." Gloria's voice trembled.

"I'm going to go kick his beep." Gordy said. "Even if he helped the wuss find a truck."

"This is between Matt and me. Mind your business. Now, go to your movie and have a good time."

They stood up to leave.

"Come on, give me a hug before you go." Gloria raised her arms.

Grudgingly, they stooped and gave her a hug. "Be careful."

As she watched them walk out the door, the phone rang. She picked up the cordless from the coffee table.

"Hello?" Gloria answered, not really wanting to talk to anyone.

"Gloria, honey, how are you? Matt called this morning and left a message for Wayne to go check on your roses. You two don't want to grow your roses together anymore?" Tanya's voice came through the phone line.

"Wayne is my regular gardener," Gloria said.

"Oh poppycock! Matt came over last weekend to borrow a doo-hickey for some yard work he was going to do and was ecstatic that Wayne had steered him your way and I'm not just talking about roses here. I haven't seen that man look so happy in years. What happened between the two of you? Not that I want to interfere or be gossipy, but, what happened?"

"Nothing."

"Maybe that's the problem." Tanya said in her usual candid way. "Make something happen, girl. I told Wayne it was a good idea. Whoops! Now, I've given myself away. Well, the cat's out of the bag. Might as well tell you the whole story. It was my idea to send Matt over to you."

"I know," Gloria said.

"Well, I knew I could never get Matt, or you, to agree to a blind date, so I convinced Wayne to send a new gardener to you, claiming he was too busy. And it almost worked, too. Are you angry?"

"No, but you know I've heard you should just let fate take its course. Your putting Matt in my path was doomed from the start because it didn't happen without a human touch."

"Oh, for the love of heaven! Neither one of you was willing to take a chance. Someone had to do it for you."

Gloria tried not to blame Tanya. She knew she meant well. But now, she was just hurt, and a hurt she could very well do without.

"I'm not giving Wayne Matt's message. So, be prepared. He feels he has to check on your roses again. If you ask me, he wants to check you out." Gloria could almost see Tanya's wide grin as she said that.

Gloria hung up and turned the TV to a Lifetime TV show, thinking that a good cry with a woman-in-jeopardy story would do wonders for her sad frame of mind. She succeeded in blocking her mind of everything, but the movie when the doorbell rang.

Gloria jumped, then her heart beat rapidly. Matt! No, it couldn't be. And it wasn't. Looking through the peephole, she saw Eddie.

"I told you not to come over here anymore." She said by way of greeting after she opened the door.

"I need to talk to you." Her ex sauntered past her and entered the house. "Do you have something to drink?"

"No." She didn't close the front door and felt the heat of the setting sun.

"This won't take long, I promise. Just need to get a few things off my chest."

"You should have called first." Gloria slammed the door shut. "I'm not up to a visit from you today."

"Oh? Trouble in paradise?" He quipped with a snide grin.

"How many times do I have to tell you that what I do, who I do it with is none of your damn business?"

"What are you doing?"

She felt her face get hot and knew she blushed. Eddie picked up on it right away. "You slept with the SOB, didn't you?"

SOB, Shortness of Breath—the term the nurses used for most of the elderly patients at Home Nursing, but she knew Eddie didn't mean that.

"Eddie..."

"How could you? After everything..." Her ex waved his hands about as he spoke.

"What do you mean 'after everything'? We've been divorced for a long time, Eddie. I should have done this a long time ago." Gloria told him, pushing aside the fact that she had never had time for a relationship with a man when the boys were little. And also, she pushed aside the fact that she had never met a man who had incited even the smallest spark of attraction—until Matt.

Eddie turned away from her and looked at the pictures of their sons on the mantel.

"Do you really want me to stay alone for the rest of my life?" Gloria demanded, even though it looked as if she might. Matt had left her and it didn't look as if he were ever coming back. Her heart lurched in her chest and she stalked to the kitchen. She opened the refrigerator and pulled out two cans of lemon-lime soda, then remembered that's what she and Matt had drunk the last time they were together. Before. She replaced the cans and retrieved two cans of cola.

"Yes, I don't want you with anyone else except me." Eddie responded standing by the dining room table.

"That's ridiculous, Eddie." She handed him the can of soda.

He popped it open, drank and didn't say a word.

"I have a right to live my life, just as you have."

"Those women don't mean a damn thing to me. They never have."

"So, why do you always go to them? You did that even when we were married. That's why we're not together anymore. Besides, we can't get along, Eddie. We argue about everything and you know it."

"Do you argue with this man?"

"No."

"You don't get angry, even a little." Eddie drank his soda again, and sank into a dining room chair. "Must be 'Mr. Perfect', huh?"

"Far from it." Gloria admitted, but remained standing. Sitting at her dining table with her ex didn't seem inviting. She stayed by the kitchen sink.

"There is trouble in paradise." Her ex looked too happy for her peace of mind and it made her want to hit him. He always evoked that feeling of violence in her, too.

"Stop being so corny." Gloria opened her soda and gulped down some of it. "Of course, we get angry, but we don't argue. We discuss."

Eddie laughed. "I remember that's what you used to tell Dex when the poor little guy yelled at us to stop fighting."

Guiltily, Gloria remembered so many scenes like that. She'd be screaming at the top of her lungs at Eddie and Dex would be crying and yelling at them to quit. "You know, not only do we argue every time we're in the same room together, but you don't bring me any good memories. Sometimes, I wonder how we managed to have two kids."

"The sex was fabulous and you know it. In the bedroom, we never had any problem." Eddie stood and before she realized it he loomed in front of her, leering, "Want to try it again? The boys aren't here. See if I can bring back those good memories for you."

Gloria shuddered and pushed him away. "Eddie, get away from me. I don't want you like that anymore. You're only the boys' father. That's the area you should work on."

"I am a good dad."

At Gloria's pointed look, he added, "Well, I try to be."

"I think you should stop trying and start doing. You really made a poor judgment in bringing that SUV over here. Poor Dex! However, Matt found him one. He's out in it right now. He and Gordy went to the movies."

Eddie ruffled his hair and looked away, walked to the living room.

Gloria followed him and found him in front of the mantel again staring at the pictures of the boys. "He found a truck for Dex?"

"Yes."

"I tried to talk to Dex earlier in the week and Gordy claimed he wasn't home."

"Maybe he wasn't. He does work, you know. Why do you think he avoided your call?"

"Because I let him down." He hung his head.

As far back as she could remember, Eddie had never admitted being in the wrong when it came to his sons.

159

"How did he manage to buy it?"

"Dex was able to pay cash for it. I helped him with the tax, title and license. I didn't want him to clean his savings out. He said he'd pay me back when he gets paid. Well, after a couple of paydays. I don't want to leave him without any spending money either."

"You're a great mom, Mrs. Amaya."

"Thank you."

"You're a great woman, too. And I never deserved you."

"So full of compliments today." Gloria smiled in spite of herself.

"Your family never liked me."

"They weren't to blame for our breakup. Don't go down that route again."

"I know. Well, I realize that now. Back then, I blamed everybody else."

"Now?"

"Well...I might have had something to do with the end of our marriage." Eddie admitted.

"Something?" Gloria repeated. "Well, I did, too. We were both too young, Eddie. And we eloped. That's not a good start. For some people, it is, but not for us. For me, I always felt guilty that I hadn't left the house in the 'right way' as my mom told me. I regret that I hurt her. A relationship as important as marriage shouldn't start with guilt."

"May I hug you?" Eddie strolled in her direction.

"No." Gloria backed away.

"For old times' sake? As a goodbye?" Eddie put his hands on her shoulders.

"Just a quick one."

Gloria felt her ex's arms go around her. The breezy smell of his cologne enveloped her. She raised her arms to hug him in return. Her body felt the solidness of his and the familiarity. However, she didn't feel anything, but what she felt when she hugged a friend. She cared for Eddie. She had loved him and borne his children. But the love was gone. And it could never be rekindled.

Eddie, on the other hand, moaned in her ear. "Oh baby, I still love you." She felt the warm breath in her ear.

She pushed him away. "If you really loved me, you

would never have cheated on me. I think you should leave."

He grinned.

"Go away."

He sobered up. "I do love you, Gloria. But, I know I lost my chance with you. And I'm not going to wish you luck with this—new man. I can't."

"Nobody knows what the future holds."

"Why isn't he here? It's Friday night."

"We...we...he was busy." Gloria evaded.

"What happened? Did he get angry with you because of me?"

Typical Eddie. Everything revolved around him. "No. It's something else."

"What?"

"I'm sick. And he can't stand illness."

Eddie's brow furrowed. "Sick? What's the matter with you?" He looked her up and down thinking he could tell what was wrong.

"I have high blood pressure." So easy to tell Eddie, but then it didn't matter so much with him.

"Is that bad?"

"Only if you don't take your medicine and eat and drink the wrong foods. It's manageable."

"So, what's his problem?"

"I told you. He has some kind of phobia about illness."

"What a wuss." Her ex pronounced, borrowing the name her sons used for each other.

She glared. "You should talk. Besides, our kids don't get along. It'll be a big mess and we'd probably wind up ending it eventually anyway."

"I'm sorry," Eddie held out his arms to her.

"I bet you are," Gloria inched further away.

Eddie walked to the front door. "As hard as it may be for you to believe, I do want you to be happy. My selfishness dictates that it be only with me, however."

"Thanks for the nice things you said to me earlier."

"I meant every word." Eddie waved and left. "Tell the boys I'll call tomorrow. I want to see Dex's new truck." Her ex opened the door.

"Why don't I just wait for you to call. I don't want

them to be disappointed."

"You don't trust me?"

"Haven't for a long time, Eddie. We'll wait for your call." Gloria shut the door.

She curled up in the armchair after Eddie left. Maybe there was hope for Eddie, to be a real dad to his sons. But, she wouldn't hold her breath. She must have dozed off because the next thing she heard was the door bell again. Were Dex and Gordy back? Not Eddie, again. It couldn't be Matt, could it? He wouldn't dare come to her doorstep without calling. Didn't he realize how dangerous that would be? She walked to the door and looked out the peephole. It was Matt. Should she open it? Maybe he would go away.

"Gloria? I heard you walk up to the door. Open it," Matt said. "Please."

If he hadn't said please, she wouldn't have opened it, she told herself.

"I had to come back. Wayne was too busy to check your roses." Matt started to walk to the backyard.

"Don't trouble yourself. I'll call Wayne later. Besides, I was just in the backyard this morning and my roses are fine. They don't need checking." Gloria put the whacking of the rose bush from her mind. "Besides, it's getting too dark to see."

Matt turned back and stared. She wore jeans and a T-shirt, her standard get-up after work and on the weekends. So, she knew he wasn't staring to take in the beauty of her appearance. "You have a light out there, don't you? Thank God, you don't have a dog in the backyard. You'd probably sic him on me," Matt said and walked away from her and around the house to the backyard.

"Come back here!" Gloria yelled and slammed the front door and ran through the living room to the patio door. "I told you I don't need you here."

Matt ignored her and went to her roses. "Turn on the light, Gloria."

He was going to see the rose bush clearly. So what? She had killed one of her rose bushes. She didn't have to explain herself. It didn't matter that he had revived them. He had also hurt her. And she wanted nothing to do with him anymore—or the rose bushes. When Wayne came to mow her yard, she would tell him to mow them down.

She flicked on the light and the backyard was illuminated. The rose bush she had hit with the rake looked wilted. Lots of rose petals were on the ground. The smell of the roses reached her as she stood at the patio door.

"What happened here?" Matt stared at the rose bush.

"Somebody killed it." She stared at him, this man who had come to mean so much to her. As she looked at him, dressed in his work shirt and jeans, the way she had seen him when she first met him, she wished they were just starting over. She would have been honest with him. But then, so should he have. What was his problem with sickness?

She looked up at the tree and it still needed trimming. But Wayne could do that. If she could just get rid of Matt—from her backyard and from her heart.

"My mom grew roses." Matt cut a pink rose off the nearest shrub.

"You told me that," Gloria said. "What does that matter now?"

He turned to her and walked toward her and handed her the rose.

Gloria refused to take it.

"I found her. Heart attack in the middle of her roses. I was thirteen. I was the first one home from school." Matt turned to her, his eyes glistening with unshed tears. "I didn't know what to do. Dad wasn't home. I ran to the neighbor and she wasn't home. I knocked at every door until I found someone. By the time the ambulance came, it was too late. Actually, they said she had been dead for hours. She probably died that morning when she went out to water her roses."

"I'm so sorry." Gloria remembered the day her mother died in the hospital. So many years later, she still remembered each thing that happened and if she told someone about it, she would be taken back to the time and place. She could only imagine the helplessness the teenaged Matt must have felt. But she refused to give in so easily. "People do get sick and some do die. What about your daughters? I'm sure they've gotten sick through the years."

"I was a wreck every time one of them so much as sniffled." He ran his fingers through his hair. A plane from the air force base nearby flew over. Then, dogs barked. "I almost lost Patsy when she was five-years-old."

Her heart went out to him. "What happened?"

"Appendicitis. However, there were complications because the doctor couldn't see the problem with the x-ray because of Patsy's fat tissue. She's always been a bit overweight. He wasn't sure it was the appendix. By the time, they did a sonogram, the appendix was on the point of rupturing. Some of the fluid got in her blood and she became septic. I'm sure you know what that is."

"She got an infection."

Matt's eyes continued to glisten. "She was a baby, my baby. I watched her day in and day out fighting for her life on that hospital bed."

"You can't go through life being afraid, Matt. Everybody gets sick. A lot of them get well."

"Some don't. Your illness scares me to death." Matt paused. "It was my fault, Gloria. I killed my mom." A tear trickled down Matt's cheek.

"What?" Her arms almost ached to hug him and tell him everything would be okay. Her maternal instinct, no doubt.

"We argued that morning before school. I'd kept harping all weekend about going on a camping trip with my friends. She didn't want to let me go. These so-called friends of mine weren't the best characters. Anyway, now I realize it. Back then, they were the cool guys and I wanted to be a part of their group. Mom insisted she wanted to meet all the boys and their parents. You can imagine what a square I would have looked." Matt smiled slightly. "Square. Where did we get these terms? What's the word nowadays? Nerd?"

"I don't know," Gloria said. "I'm sorry."

"I told her I hated her, that she was ruining my life and that as soon as I was sixteen, I was going to quit school and never visit her again. I ran out of the house and I could hear her calling to me. 'Matt, *mijo*, we'll talk about it when you get home. Maybe we can work something out. *Mijito!*' And then, I come home and she's dead. I never went on that damn camping trip."

"I bet you haven't gone camping period."

"How did you know?" Matt's head dropped to his chest.

"You can't avoid life forever."

"Is that what you think I'm doing?"

"Aren't you?"

Matt looked at the drooping rose bush. "You won't need to fertilize the roses until the spring. Don't forget to water them, though, at least once a week."

Gloria stared at the rose bush, too. "Thank you for reviving my roses."

Matt stared at the rosebush, then at her and walked toward her with his arms outstretched.

She stepped back and stepped on the rake's prongs. With a yell, she felt the prong stick into her sole. "Ouch!"

Matt helped her toward the patio table. "Are you hurt?"

"A little." She threw her shoe off and grabbed her foot to rub it. "See, anything can happen at anytime. How can you stop bad things from happening?"

Before Gloria could stop him, he grabbed her foot and massaged it. When she would have wrenched it away, he tightened his grip. As he continued the massage, she felt her blood singing.

"Stop that. Now." She squirmed so he would let her go.

He released her foot.

Matt put his head on her lap. "You're going to die."

"Not this minute I'm not. I've got too much to live for still. And I'm taking care of myself. That's all I can do, Matt."

"I love you," Matt whispered into her lap.

Gloria's heart lifted at his words. "Love?" However, he had hurt her with his actions and words. "You have a fine way of showing it."

"I fell in love with you in a matter of days among your roses." Matt grabbed her face with both hands. "I'm sorry. This past week has been hell on me, and I bet for you, too."

Gloria's eyes filled with tears. "I'm sorry I didn't tell you about my high blood pressure. I think I knew you had a problem. You stiffened up at the mention of illness. But, I should have come clean, as my sons say."

"You know when I brought over the truck for Dex and you said sometimes things are too good to be true?"

She nodded.

"That's when I realized I had found the real thing. Someone too good to be true, but she was that good. And I couldn't let you go."

"Oh Matt." Gloria lay her head on his shoulder. "It is a good thing. We'll work it out. With our kids, with our exes, with everything. If we really want to."

"I want to." Matt kissed her. "Where are your sons, by the way?" Matt peeked in through the patio door.

"They went to the movies."

Matt smiled and kissed her again.

Gloria put her arms around his neck. "I'm so glad you came back. But now, you're going to have to face the music with my sons. I've been crying ever since last night so they know something is wrong."

"I'll talk to them."

"You might have to sign a contract in blood, too, something along the lines that you'll never hurt their mom again."

"I'll do my best not to do that."

And as the sun set even more in the west, Gloria knew that in the morning, the sun would rise again on a new day for both her and Matt, her family and—her roses.

A word about the author...

L. M. Gonzalez lives in South Texas with her two sons. She obtained a degree in Business Administration because her dad advised her to "get a trade". However, in 1976 she wrote her first story and has continued writing stories since then. In 2001 she joined Romance Writers of America and her local. This was the year that she decided to pursue publication of her stories. L. M. loves to write stories about Latinas, their lives and their loves, as well as about motherhood and single parenting.

Visit L.M.'s site at www.freewebs.com/lesmora